THE SECRETS OF ISLAYNE

KARI LYNN WEST

Copyright © 2017 by Kari Lynn West

All rights reserved. No part of this publication may be reproduced, distributed, or transmitted in any form or by any means, including photocopying, recording, or other electronic or mechanical methods, without the prior written permission of the publisher, except in the case of brief quotations embodied in critical reviews and certain other noncommercial uses permitted by copyright law.

Printed in the United States of America

First Edition, 2017

www.karilynnwest.com

This is a work of fiction. Names, characters, places, and incidents either are the products of the author's imagination or are used fictitiously. Any resemblance to actual persons, living or dead, businesses, companies, events, or locales is entirely coincidental.

Cover design by Ebook Launch

❀ Created with Vellum

to jason,
for courage, stolen time, all the red ink,
& a shared love of stories.
this book wouldn't exist without you,
& I'm glad I don't have to, either.

PROLOGUE

MEMORIES ARE SACRED. MEMORIES ARE SACRED. MEMORIES ARE SACRED. The words kept flitting around his mind like insistent flies—inconsequential, but no less annoying—as he steered the small motor boat toward the mouth of the cave. That mantra was the foundational tenet of lumination; it had no place on his nighttime journey. Luminators lived to bring memories back from the brink of extinction. Never to push them over the edge. It was unthinkable; it was impossible.

More fool them.

The boat coasted up to the shore. It was dark, but he'd come prepared. He retrieved the book, flashlight, and battery-powered standing lamps and carried them deep into the cave. He wound his way through seemingly endless passageways, hearing only the fall of his footsteps and the far-away drip of water on stone. Finally, he turned the last sharp corner of the twisting tunnel and stepped into a large cavern. The flashlight cast a narrow beam of light, pale and weak, into the dark expanse, as if at any moment it could be swallowed up by shadow. During the day, the chamber was beautiful. There was no daylight now.

He walked to a long, high bench in the middle of the stone floor and placed one lamp on either side. He took a moment to gaze down at the book in his hands and trace the strange markings on the leather cover. Even though Classical Gaelic wasn't something they taught at the Academy, he'd slowly deciphered the text. For years, he struggled against the power of those translated words; it didn't matter in the end though. In an instant, desperation and grief brought a vicious clarity to his life, and the knowledge burrowed deep within him blossomed into something vital and beautiful. Why should he serve the cause of memories when they'd only ever brought him despair? Better to break them to his will.

He glanced down at his watch. For a moment, Elise's smiling face rose up in his memory. He recalled her barely contained excitement as she placed the watch in his hands, eager to see his reaction to the birthday present. He pushed the thought firmly away. This wasn't the time.

They would be here any moment. He waited, relishing the perfect stillness all around him. It wouldn't last much longer. Soon enough, screams would drive out the silence.

1

For the tenth time that day, Ronan Saunders pulled the letter out from his pocket just to make sure it still existed. Even though he'd received the response yesterday, he still couldn't bear to have it out of reach. This was his chance. Now he could finally prove himself. He touched the return address in the upper left-hand corner of the envelope:

Andrew Angler
Senior Luminator
51 Linton Avenue
Lumin District, Islayne

After four years of grueling work at the Academy and nine months of writing inquiries, he finally had an apprenticeship.

Ronan put the letter back and looked up at the large clock hung on the opposite wall of the bookshop. 7:15 p.m. Why hadn't Mr. Isaacson come out of his office yet? Normally, Ronan wouldn't care. But today was different; today, he could finally tell his boss that he was quitting *Third Street Books*.

Ronan had tried to share his news with Mr. Isaacson right when he got to the bookstore earlier that afternoon, but Ronan had been ten minutes late to his shift. When he finally arrived, his boss had just glared at him and then mumbled something about balancing sales reports before holing himself up in his back office for the rest of the day. So Ronan had waited. And waited. Of course the man would choose this day of all days to change up his evening routine.

Mr. Isaacson always walked out of the back office an hour before closing time, told Ronan exactly how to lock up, warned him about time theft, and then left grumbling about how today's teenagers had no work ethic. When he was safely out of earshot, Ronan normally grumbled back that today's bookstore owners, at least one in particular, had forgotten the very important role of breath mints in any working relationship.

But, bad breath aside, Ronan couldn't fault him for his complaints. Today marked the fifth time that Ronan had arrived late for his shift. He'd also fallen asleep twice during customer lulls—which were quite frequent— and once he'd alphabetized all the new arrivals by the author's first name. He wasn't trying to be bad at his job, but there were days when he couldn't seem to keep his mind engaged in the task at hand. Ronan was sure he would have been out of a job by now if his mum wasn't such good friends with Mr. Isaacson's wife. So he thought his news would come as a relief to both of them. Ronan knew the man's patience was wearing thin.

The problem wasn't with his work ethic though, despite what his employer thought. Ronan had poured himself into his studies for four years, from age twelve until sixteen, and graduated last August near the top of his class at the Academy, the premier (and only) school for luminators. The problem was he could only seem to apply his work ethic to things that mattered to him. Working at a bookstore, especially a used bookstore, didn't make the shortlist. He liked new books with fresh ink pressed into crisp, sweet-smelling pages. Old ones grossed him out. He hated the feel of deterioration at his fingertips, and he couldn't help but think about how many other hands the books had passed through before finding their way into his. It was like eating a stranger's leftovers.

It wasn't just the old books, though, that made this job difficult. Each day that he walked into this small, dusty, often-deserted place, it felt like he was taking a step backwards from what he was supposed to be doing. The whole point of the lumination trade was to bring old memories back to life;

this store just continued to decline. Maybe other people felt aimless after graduating high school, but Ronan had the opposite problem. He couldn't bring himself to care about any other kind of work when he had the ability to revive other people's memories. Why would he want to use his hands to shelve books when he could use his mind to give someone back a restored piece of the forgotten past?

Ronan glanced at the overstuffed, disorganized bookshelves and then back up to the clock. Still no sign of his boss. He fidgeted with the front display signs. Even though *Third Street Books* was one of only two bookstores on the whole island of Islayne, it wasn't exactly a hub of excitement on a Thursday evening, or any other evening, for that matter. With no browsing customers, Ronan could clearly hear the ancient air conditioning unit whirring at the back of the room. Even the air here was old and stagnant. Ronan knew he should start sorting through the last donation box, but he felt too on edge. He was beyond ready to be out of here. He wanted to slam the door on these last nine months and never look back.

Ever since he manifested the gifting at age twelve, lumination was the only thing he wanted to do. It wasn't just that he believed the work was worthwhile; it was that he felt worthless without the work. Whenever he was on holiday from school, he'd start to feel aimless and out-of-sorts. Academy life was grueling and often tedious, but since Ronan knew it was a necessary step toward earning his practicing license, he felt content there. Working toward the day he could become a fully-fledged luminator was the only way to calm the restlessness inside him.

The bell at the front of the bookstore rang, announcing a new customer. Ronan looked up and groaned inwardly. Kendrick Lydon. There was only one reason the giant of a sixteen-year-old would set foot in this bookstore, and it wasn't to improve his mind. If he wanted to read, he could pick up any of the books from his father's massive private library. But Ronan had a hunch he didn't spend much time in there, either.

With broad shoulders, curly light brown hair, and a face that could have been carved from stone, Kendrick looked like he'd stepped out of a Greek myth. And since many of the characters in Greek mythology were arrogant, cruel, and annoying, he would have fit in well. He'd somehow managed to graduate from the same Academy class as Ronan, a feat some attributed more to his father's influence over certain professors than Kendrick's dedication to his studies. What he lacked in talent or hard work, he made up for in power, wealth, and condescension. Once he found out that Ronan was working here, he'd been stopping by at least once a week to brag about his lumination apprenticeship, pull out dozens of books and leave them scattered in random piles along the aisles, and in general find any way to make Ronan's work just that much more miserable.

"Oh, Ronan, you're here today?" Kendrick asked, feigning innocence as he walked up to the cash register. "The name tag suits you." He smirked.

Ronan took a deep breath. He reminded himself that he was almost done working here and his apprenticeship would begin in just over a week. He could handle Kendrick; he was not going to let his obnoxious classmate bait him again.

"Can I help you find something?" Ronan asked, keeping his voice level.

"Well, aren't we the helpful little book clerk. Trying to win employee of the month? Get the best parking spot?"

"Just here to serve," Ronan said, fighting to keep the sarcasm out of his voice.

"Isn't that sweet," Kendrick said, leaning back on the front display table. He grinned at Ronan, and then flipped the table backwards, sending books hurtling to the floor.

"What the *hell?*" Ronan yelled, wholly abandoning his plan to stay calm. "Why would you do—" But then he heard the office door open.

"What's going on? Ronan is that you yelling?" Mr. Isaacson called from the back of the store.

Ronan took a deep breath. "It's nothing sir," he answered. "A customer accidentally knocked something over."

"Well, clean it up," his boss said, and then Ronan heard the office door slam shut. He mumbled a few expletives under his breath as he walked around the register and began to pick up the books and stack them on a nearby table.

"Manners, manners," Kendrick said. "I don't think that's any way to talk with a customer around. You're going to have to work on these things if you hope to make it in the bookselling trade. But then again, maybe you like failing at things. You are good at it."

"Yeah? I'm pretty sure the class rankings at the Academy told a different story," Ronan said, bending down to collect the display signs.

"I'm glad passing some tests made you feel good. It'll be a nice thing for you to remember when you're still shelving books in twenty years."

"You wouldn't know how passing tests made me feel since you never did the same."

"I'm just glad no one takes those marks too seriously, or who knows how polluted the trade would become?" Right as Ronan flipped the table back over, Kendrick grabbed hold of the edge to keep it off balance. "You might have been able to worm your way into the Academy, but in the real world, people still know the value of blood."

"You know what I think is funny?" Ronan asked, yanking the table out of Kendrick's grasp. "That all these luminators, completely unrelated to you, are starting to do so well in the trade. It's a little sad, seeing all you washed-up, inbred pricks start to lose your hold on the one thing you've ever been halfway good at doing."

Ronan saw Kendrick's hands ball into fists, but then he relaxed them again. "I spend my days training with Denison, and you spend yours dusting off books that nobody reads. You tell me which of us is on track for a stellar career."

Even with the acceptance letter in his pocket, Ronan couldn't help but feel the same twinge of envy he always experienced at the thought of Kendrick training with Justus Denison, one of the top-ranked luminators on the island—to which Ronan had written three inquiries with no response. The idea left a bitter taste in his mouth.

Those nine months of sending out fruitless apprenticeship applications had been the most frustrating season of Ronan's life, made worse by the fact that he'd only had one year to find an apprenticeship after graduating. If the luminator ability wasn't utilized at least once a year, then it would fade out from lack of practice, like a muscle fully atrophied from disuse. The thought of a future without lumination was enough to make him sick, but as the months wore on with nothing changing, he began to lose hope of ever finding a place in the trade.

With each rejection letter Ronan opened, he would think back to the phrase so often repeated by Professor Blenchel, the smug, belittling woman who taught luminator history at the Academy. *Lumination is like fine wine—it only gets better with age.* And by age, she meant generations. For centuries, luminators had stemmed from one main, wealthy family on Islayne, the Lydons, and two other smaller branches of that family, the Brenningtons and the Roscoes.

But the luminator power wasn't in the families' blood; it was in their land. They had owned the entire northeastern section of the island, now called the Lumin District, and there was *something* in that part of the land that gave a portion of its residents the power to see and restore other people's memories. No one knew what it was exactly about the land that awoke this ability, but any luminator who moved to a different part of the island or anywhere else in the world soon found that their powers didn't work, and if he or she didn't move back to the land, the gifting soon died out completely.

But the land and the power it bestowed apparently hadn't been enough to supply the Lydons' lavish lifestyles. In the late 1890s, they defaulted on a massive loan, and the bank seized a portion of the land that had been put up as collateral. Several years after developers turned the land into smaller homes and neighborhoods, a few of the children of the new residents began to show an uncanny knack for sensing memories. And soon enough, those children wanted a place in the lumination world.

The old families were furious over the advent of new luminators, or what they called the *bastardization of their trade*, though Ronan never understood how it could have come as a surprise. He thought it would be next to impossible for anyone to have this gifting and not want to use it. Regardless, the members of the old families made sure these outside luminators felt every inch of their disdain, and they did everything in their power to keep newer blood from being successful in the trade.

Ronan's grandparents had purchased a home in one of the neighborhoods on the northeastern side of the island. As the only one in his graduating class of fifteen students that was not related to the Lydons, the Brenningtons, or the Roscoes, Ronan had faced his fair share of prejudice from professors and other students at the Academy. Professor Blenchel, who happened to be a distant cousin of the Brenningtons, had done her best to treat Ronan as a second-class citizen for daring to have the gifting without a drop of the old families' blood in his veins, no matter that his own family had been on Islayne for generations, and on the Scottish mainland for ages before that. Once when he'd answered a question wrong, she'd smirked and replied, "Well, what can one expect of a common islander?" As if to say that if Ronan truly took the trade seriously, he would've found a way to change his lineage.

These kind of comments often made Ronan want to punch his teacher in her small, pinched face. But since he valued his Academy education, and he knew he would *eventually* feel guilty for hitting a middle-aged woman, instead he channeled all of his frustration into learning everything there was to know about the history of lumination, making sure he didn't give his professor any more openings for snide remarks. This was how he responded in general to the suspicion, derision, or outright hostility of anyone at the Academy, and it was how he graduated near the top of his class. But in the months following, as he wrote enquiry after enquiry and received rejection after rejection, Ronan began to wonder if he'd done enough.

And in all that time, rich, spoiled brats like Kendrick received apprenticeships they hadn't earned and didn't appreciate, as if it were their due, simply because they shared a certain last name.

"How many Council members did your dad have to pay off to get Denison interested in you?" Ronan asked. "Or wait, let me guess, did your mum convince him with her *special* kind of persuasion?"

Kendrick's eyes flashed in anger, and he took a menacing step toward Ronan. At that moment, the back office door opened again, and Mr. Isaacson walked toward them. His shoulders were hunched as if against the cold, though it was at least seventy degrees in the store. He had one of those weathered faces that made it both impossible to tell exactly how old he was and hard to imagine that he had ever been young. He wore his normal scowl as he walked up to the register, taking in the mess and Kendrick's presence.

"I don't pay you to hang out with your friends," he told Ronan gruffly.

"He's not a friend," Ronan replied.

Without a word, Kendrick turned on his heel and disappeared back down one of the crowded aisles of the store. Ronan thought he'd probably have a few dozen more books to clean up before he was done today.

Mr. Isaacson frowned toward Kendrick before turning to face Ronan. "No other customers?" he asked, the accusation clear in his voice.

Oh yes, Ronan thought. *Loads of them. Until I started dancing naked through the history and biography sections. For some reason, the bibliophiles didn't take to my customer engagement strategy.*

"No sir," he said out loud. "It's been pretty quiet for the past hour. But I wanted to say—"

"Well, you should know the routine by now," Mr. Isaacson spoke as if he hadn't heard Ronan, which was a definite possibility. "Bring all the sale books in from the front right at 8 o'clock, and—"

"Before we go over all of that again," Ronan interjected, louder this time. "I need to tell you something."

"Well boy, out with it. I don't have all night."

Even though Ronan had been looking forward to this moment all day, he wished Kendrick had left first. Knowing he would overhear this conversation somehow made it feel less satisfying.

"I'm quitting," he said. "I can only give you a week's notice. I'm sorry it's not longer, but I just accepted a lumination apprenticeship yesterday, so I'll be starting that soon."

Mr. Isaacson stared at him for a moment. Ronan realized that he actually had no idea how his employer felt about the trade; islanders tended to fall into one of a few different groups when it came to their thoughts on lumination. Some worshipped luminators and saw them as their very own homegrown celebrities. Others thought the trade was unimportant, a luxury of the rich, while they had real businesses to run, families to feed, and lives to live. Then there were the one-off nut jobs who still saw luminators as unnatural and feared their power, even with how long the trade had existed and with all the many Lumin Council regulations in place.

His boss snorted in derision. "And here I thought you'd finally come to your senses, getting some experience in the real world instead of dreaming about some fancy, lazy excuse for a job."

Ah, so he's the second sort, Ronan thought. *It could be worse. At least he's not one of the few who'd still like to burn me at the stake.*

Ronan was used to the fact that a lot of people, like his parents, didn't understand why lumination was so appealing to those who had the gifting, and he wasn't about to waste his time trying to convince someone like Mr. Isaacson of why he'd prefer an apprenticeship to this dead-end job.

"Sorry to disappoint," Ronan said, not sounding at all sorry. "I'll still lock up tonight, of course, and be here for the next week."

"Be sure you do it properly," Mr. Isaacson said, walking toward the front door. "No sloppiness. But don't bother coming in any more after tonight. Not when you don't have the common sense to know when you're giving up a good thing."

And with that, he left. Ronan shook his head. He guessed it would have been too much to hope that his boss would have shared in his excitement. At least now he was only minutes away from being done with this place once and for all. And speaking of being done with things…

"Kendrick! We're closing soon—don't you have anything better to do than stay here and annoy me?"

Kendrick materialized from the back aisle of the store. He looked like he'd gotten over Ronan's insult to his mom. In fact, he looked ecstatic.

"Well, well, let me be the first to congratulate you. It looks like you're finally moving up in the world."

"Yeah, I can tell that's very heartfelt," Ronan said. "How about you congratulate me by leaving?"

"Oh sure, just, wait one second. What did I do with that letter?" He made a show of checking his coat pockets before finally pulling a crisp, clean envelope from the inside of his jacket and placing it on the counter in front of him.

"Remember the phrase, Ronan? *Lumination is like fine wine.* When will you all ever learn? I think you'll want to read this. I managed to convince one of the Council members who owed my dad a favor to let me deliver it to you myself. I told him it'd be better coming from me, since we were classmates and everything. It'd make it easier on you." His smile was positively gleeful.

Ronan ripped open the envelope and unfolded the piece of paper inside. The Lumin Council's official seal was stamped in the bottom right hand corner. He scanned the letter.

We regret to inform you that the Council has invalidated your recent acceptance...

Sen. Andrew Angler has failed to maintain his luminator license...

He is unfit for training at this time...

The words swam in front of him. He couldn't finish reading.

"The cheap stuff might look pretty in a bottle, Ronan, but those with good taste will still spit it out."

Ronan barely registered Kendrick's words. He barely heard the bell ring as he left. Everything felt far away, and nothing could drown out the roaring in his head.

2

"Did you hear me?"

Failed, failed, failed, unfit, unfit, unfit. Ronan read the words over and over, saying them under his breath, until they didn't feel like words anymore. They were just markings on a page, sounds in the air. They didn't mean anything. They couldn't take his future from him. Not if he just kept repeating them. He could make them meaningless.

"Hey! Are you on something?"

He looked up from the counter, and a girl's face slowly came into focus. She had curly brown hair, freckles, and green eyes, narrowed in annoyance. Something about her appearance looked familiar to Ronan, but he thought he'd probably just seen that same look of annoyance mirrored in the faces of other customers over the past few months.

"So, do you?" she asked, sounding exasperated, and placed her hands on her…very nicely curved hips.

"Do I what?"

"Have any tourist guides here?" Her tone made it clear that it was not the first time she'd asked her question. Yes, she was definitely annoyed at him. Maybe on some other day, he would have cared. But not today. Of course, he should get used to this. Helping frustrated customers find tourist guides was going to be his life now. Well, not here, since he didn't have a job here after tonight. But there was that one other bookstore on the island. He could learn to be a *book clerk extraordinaire* there, and wow everyone with his talents. What a bright future awaited him. He started laughing uncontrollably.

"Okay, you are on something. Is there someone else here who can actually help me?"

"Nope," he said, getting his laughter under control. "Just me. I'm the only one in the world right now who can show you where we keep the tourist guides. Doesn't that make me special? One of a kind, you might say."

"Crazy, you might say."

"I guess it all depends on your perspective."

"Whatever. Listen, I'm stuck on this godforsaken island for the entire summer, and the only person I know here won't be out of school for a few more days. I'd like to try to figure out if there's anything even remotely new and interesting to do in the meantime, so can you just pull yourself together long enough to point me in the right direction?"

She was complaining about a three-month holiday. Ronan's whole future was slipping away from him, and this girl was pissed because she had to spend the summer in one of the most beautiful places in the world. Godforsaken island, seriously? Had she seen any of Islayne's views? It wasn't some kind of tropical paradise since it was sixty miles off the coast of Scotland, but that made it even better. It was unique and breathtaking. She was just another rich, spoiled brat who didn't appreciate the life she'd been given. She'd fit right in with Kendrick.

Third Street Books had a large selection of tourist guides since visitors often didn't want to keep them after their stay. It became a kind of tradition for people to donate them to one of the two used bookstores before they left. Ronan thought she must not even have tried to look for herself. They weren't that hard to find. He went over to the right bookshelf, grabbed an armful of them, and unceremoniously dropped them on the floor in front of the girl. She jumped back as one of them hit her foot.

"Ouch! What is wrong with you?"

"Just here to help," he said. "And it's not a godforsaken island. People come here from all over the world."

"Must be for the incredible customer service," she muttered as she pulled one of the books out at random and put it on the counter. She didn't even look at the cover or compare it to any of the other ones. Rich and not too bright. She'd definitely be a good match for Kendrick.

"That'll be eight pounds," he said.

She handed over a ten pound note.

"Sorry, exact change only. It's past seven. Store policy."

"I don't have exact change, and I'm pretty sure you just made that up."

"Sorry. Like I said, store policy. There's nothing I can do."

The girl stood there for a moment, and Ronan wondered if she was debating whether or not to throw the book at his head. Instead, she chose to drop it back on the floor and then left without another word.

"Welcome to Islayne! Hope you enjoy your stay!" he called as she walked out the door.

Ronan knew he should probably feel guilty for taking his frustration out on a stranger, but he didn't. She insulted his home. The only thing worse was insulting his trade. Oh but wait, it wasn't his trade. Not anymore. If the Lydons could get to Angler, then he didn't have a chance in hell at ever finding an apprenticeship. His gifting would die out. All the frustration came rushing back to him as he locked up the bookstore and made his way back home.

Ten minutes later, he parked his car in the driveway, grabbed the stack of letters and magazines from the mailbox, and walked into the kitchen. The silence in the house felt comforting for the first time since his parents had left to visit family on the mainland the previous week. Instead of feeling lonely, Ronan only felt relieved that he didn't have to share his bad news immediately. His parents, who were both high school teachers, hadn't been off of Islayne in a few years, and they were planning on staying away for most of the summer. They had been hesitant about leaving him on his own while they were gone, but he'd sold them on the fact that he was being responsible in his job. The job he'd just quit. That was going to go over *really* well when he told them.

Well, at least his mother would be relieved that his one chance at lumination had slammed shut in his face. Though the Academy focused on developing luminator abilities, students still took all the normal high school classes—and in four years instead of six—in case they couldn't make it in the luminator world. His mother had pleaded with him to look into other jobs or to apply to colleges on the mainland after a few months of futile apprenticeship applications. He always detected a note of relief in her voice during these conversations, since the fact that they had to have them at all meant he wasn't making any headway in the field. It frustrated him, but a part of him understood her feelings. Lumination was highly dangerous to practice; he couldn't blame his mum for wanting him to become a professor or an accountant or anything that didn't run such a high risk of, well, dying. But to Ronan, doing anything else would be settling for a less interesting, less impactful life. That's why he could never bring himself to consider other career paths.

Well, I should probably start now, he thought dejectedly as he grabbed a bag of potato crisps from the pantry and began to sort through the junk mail and brightly-colored catalogues, looking for anything to distract him from the fact that his whole future just went up in smoke. Near the back of the pile, he found a small letter. There was no return address on the envelope, and the writing was barely legible, so much so that Ronan was surprised the mailman was able to decipher his name and address. He tore open the envelope and pulled out a crumpled piece of paper. It read:

I'll train you. Be at my office next Monday. 6 a.m. – Ben Roscoe

Was this some kind of joke? He imagined Kendrick stopping by his house and slipping this letter into the mailbox, adding even more insult to injury. But though the page was rumpled and stained, Ronan recognized it as the heavy, textured paper the Council gave to luminator offices to conduct official correspondence, and he could see Ben Roscoe's office address embossed at the top center of the page.

Ronan stared at the paper. There was no official acceptance letter. No contract detailing the terms of his service. No formal congratulations. Just a scrawled note. A seeming afterthought. But it was an afterthought that could change everything. Ronan had been sure he would never get the chance to train under any luminator, ever. Now, strange as it was, here was one more invitation.

There was only one problem. Everyone knew that Ben Roscoe was crazy.

3

"Eli, hold the ladder still!" Cassie called down from where she was perched outside the second-story window. She might be an adrenaline junkie, but no one *wanted* to fall fifteen feet and risk breaking a leg.

"If you spent less time yelling at me and more time waking him up, you could have already been back down by now!" Eli shouted up to her.

"Well I can't wake him up if you shake me off this ladder, and I fall on your head," she answered.

"Actually yeah, that would probably create enough noise to do the trick," he replied and rattled the ladder slightly.

"That's not funny!" she yelled, gripping the metal rungs in front of her, but she couldn't quite keep the smile out of her voice. She steadied herself and reached out to knock on the window, but at that moment the glass pane slid up, revealing a very annoyed-looking Ronan. His black hair was mussed from sleep.

"Oh those are cute," she said, taking in his pajamas. "*Star Wars*, huh?"

"Cassie," he groaned, raking his fingers through his hair. "It's midnight. I'm tired. I thought we'd grown out of this tradition."

"That's the point of traditions, silly, you don't grow out of them. We have to celebrate. Today was my *last day* of ever being a fifth year. The summer has officially begun! And this time, it will be particularly special.

C'mon, get dressed. Before Eli starts complaining about muscle cramps again."

Eli shook the ladder for emphasis.

"My parents know we do this every year, and they aren't even here this time," Ronan said. "Couldn't you have just used the front door? It's not like you don't know where we keep the spare key."

She rolled her eyes. "You have no sense of adventure. This is part of the fun."

"You know I hate heights, right? And ladders?"

"Face your fears, Saunders. You'll never get anywhere in life otherwise."

"If I climb down, will you promise to stop lecturing me?"

Her grin widened. "I thought you'd never ask."

A moment later, she stepped off the lowest ladder rung and joined Eli in front of Ronan's house. Thick, luscious trees pressed in at the edges of the small green lawn. She pulled her jacket closer against the cool nighttime air. The light from the full moon filtered in through the nearby branches to dance in strange patterns on the ground. She closed her eyes for a moment and breathed in deeply, savoring the faint salty tang of the sea air. She could hear the wind rustling the leaves of the forest. Islayne was always beautiful, but the island seemed to weave a particular kind of enchantment over Cassie's heart at night.

She opened her eyes and caught Eli looking at her, his dark eyes reflecting bits of the moonlight, his expression unreadable.

"Okay, yes, I'm a little weird," she said. "You can stop staring at me now."

He ducked his head and didn't say anything. Which was strange. Eli Brennington rarely ran out of words. He and Cassie were similar in that regard. It was one of the reasons they spent half of their friendship arguing.

Ronan finally climbed out of the window and carefully made his way down the ladder.

"Hurry up," Eli complained. "My arms are starting to ache." But he didn't shake the ladder this time; it was a wise decision, since most likely, Ronan really would have lost his balance and fallen on top of Eli.

When Ronan reached the ground, he turned to Eli. "What is so hard about holding a ladder?"

"Okay, you're right. I wasn't tired. But it was so boring down here by myself that I had to think of some way to get you guys to hurry. Reminded me too much of the time Cassie wanted to explore that condemned luminator office at the edge of the district, and I had to stand watch for *hours*."

"Oh, it wasn't that long," Cassie said dismissively.

"Either way, that's still better than what Cass made me do last year when we had to break you out of your mansion," Ronan said. "Have you ever tried to climb up that lattice in the back? It is not as easy as it looks. And if your parents had caught me, they wouldn't have been nearly as forgiving as mine."

"Then it's a good thing they sleep like the dead," Eli said. "I think it's the weight of ten generations of polite backstabbing and pretension. Must be bloody exhausting for them to carry that around all the time."

"I don't know what either of you are complaining about," Cassie said, rummaging around in her backpack until she found her flashlight. "You both had the easy job in either plan. I was the only one in real danger."

"Yeah, but you also created the plan, so whose fault was that?" Eli countered. "You know, for being an adrenaline junkie, you were born on the wrong island. Should have been Australian or something."

Cassie snorted derisively. "It doesn't take any imagination to have adventures in Australia. I like to think up my own fun, thanks. Keeps me sharp."

"I don't know if I'd go that far," Ronan said, raising his eyebrows. Cassie feigned throwing her flashlight at his head.

She glanced between her two friends. Tall and lanky, Eli had unruly light blond hair and the almost-black eyes and fair skin that ran in most of the older families on the island. Ronan, on the other hand, had a shorter, more compact frame, dark hair, and light grey eyes. Cassie often thought that he looked like Eli's inverse, and their differences didn't end with their appearances. Though they both had the lumination gifting, since Eli was the only son of one of the wealthiest and oldest families on the island, Cassie still found it incredible that the two of them had become such good friends at the Academy. She knew that Eli's parents despised Ronan for trying to become a luminator, but it never seemed to affect Eli's view of him. In fact, Cassie suspected that it made him like Ronan even more.

It was a good thing that Eli didn't often let his parents' prejudice sway him, because otherwise he would have never befriended her. Though she didn't have the gifting (and didn't want it), her father, Alister Murdoch, was the most famous and most successful new luminator on Islayne. If there was anyone that the Brenningtons despised, it was her dad and anyone related to him.

Cassie was definitely related to him, though sometimes, it barely felt that way. The old families may have hated him, but her father was a hero and an inspiration to most of the new luminators on Islayne—including Ronan. Not only did he symbolize all that they could achieve, but her father spent a good chunk of his time and money campaigning for a Council seat, wanting to bring more fairness to the trade and curb the corrupting influence of the old families. He fought for the rights of strangers, and in exchange, forfeited time with his only daughter.

Cassie immediately felt guilty and immature for the thought. *Stop whining*, she told herself. *You're not a child; you don't need a babysitter.* But deep down, she knew that part of the reason she could be so reckless, part of the reason she planned these crazy summer escapades with Ronan and Eli, was out of the hope that one night, she would sneak back home at 2 a.m. to find her father waiting up for her. She imagined her father lecturing her and doling out consequences for being out so late and scaring him half to death.

But so far, she'd always come back to a quiet house.

Maybe it wasn't his fault. Maybe her mum would have been the worrier for both of them. She couldn't blame him for the fact that her mum had died from a brain aneurism just a few days before Cassie's sixth birthday.

"We should go," she said, pushing away thoughts of her parents as she started walking toward the dirt road at the edge of Ronan's yard.

"Can't we just drive there like we drove here?" Eli asked, gesturing toward Cassie's jeep parked in Ronan's driveway.

"No questions," Cassie said, continuing toward the path. "You'd think after three summers, you would remember the rules."

"And you'd think after three summers, you wouldn't be such a control freak," Eli muttered.

"I heard that," Cassie called back over her shoulder. After walking along the main road for a few minutes, she led them down a path they'd used countless times in the past few years. It meandered through the wooded area around Ronan's house, then led up a long, steep incline to a clearing where multiple hiking trails fanned out, spanning a good portion of the north side of the island.

As they made their way through the woods, Cassie's mind wandered back to the first time she'd met Ronan and Eli. Three and a half years ago, the headmaster of the Academy had invited her father to speak to the students about his lumination career. Cassie remembered her father's furrowed brow as he read the official invitation; most at the Academy despised him. But he was in the midst of another campaign, so he couldn't pass up the chance to garner publicity. He accepted.

He should have ripped the fancy card to shreds instead.

Cassie recalled the excitement she'd felt as they drove up to the entrance of the Academy, the afternoon sun painting streaks of light on the worn stone of the castle walls. Originally an old fortress supposedly built by one of the Lords of the Isles centuries ago, the old families had renovated the building and started the Academy here in the late 1800s. Most people thought the building impressive, but Cassie couldn't care less. Her enthusiasm had nothing to do with where she was; it had everything to do with the person sitting next to her.

She treasured times like that drive, when her father was cheerful, attentive, and relaxed. Most days, he was so focused on his work or his campaign, he didn't have much time to spare. And in the leftover moments of the day that he did spend with her, he was often distracted and exhausted. But that morning, he'd *seen* her. It almost made up for how he'd acted afterward.

Everything seemed to go smoothly at first. The headmaster was there at the front of the school to greet them. He was pleasant and bland, guiding them back to the main assembly hall. She didn't know if he'd intended to humiliate her father, or if he was just an idiot, thinking the rest of the school would fall in line with his good intentions. Either way, he'd been no help. The whole student body was already gathered when they walked into the hall. Cassie could still clearly recall the high ceilings, painted purple, and feel the weight of the stares of close to a hundred people as she followed her father toward the front of the room, and then took a seat off by herself to the left of the stage.

The students were quiet as the headmaster introduced her father, and no one moved to clap as Alister took the microphone. But as soon as he began his speech, that silence ended. Kids started whispering, snickering, opening books, rustling papers, and a few even stood up and started moving around. Some were paying attention, but for the majority, it was as if no one was on stage at all. None of the teachers made any move to reign in their students, and some even joined in the disruption.

At first, her father tried to carry on with his speech, ignoring the noise, but the room got steadily louder and louder. Then as if on cue, about a dozen students from various places in the audience stood up and threw crumbled up pieces of paper toward the front of the room. Cassie stared, horrified, as two of the paper balls hit her dad in the face as he was talking, and the rest littered the stage. He broke off mid-sentence, and Cassie could see the hurt and fury warring in her father's face. Abruptly, he turned aside and stormed off the stage, rushing straight past Cassie and pushing though the auditorium doors. Applause filled the hall as he left. Cassie froze for a moment, unsure how to act as the students continued their mocking ovation. Then she jumped up and chased after her father, the shame and outrage churning in her stomach, but as she rushed out the front doors of the building, she saw her father's silver Lexus speeding away down the driveway.

He'd left her behind. She stared as her father's car became a small speck in the distance. She tried to tell herself it was just an accident, it could happen to anyone, that surely he'd realize his mistake and be back any minute. But the minutes passed, and no silver Lexus drove back toward her.

Days later, he took her out to dinner and apologized profusely. He explained how he'd been so angry that he couldn't think straight. He promised that he would never do something like that again. And she would try to tell herself the same things she'd told him—that it wasn't a big deal and she understood.

But in that moment, as she stared out at the empty road in front of her, it was a big deal. And she did not understand.

"Wow, you must have a *lot* of trouble reading social cues," said a voice behind her. "All of that in there meant, 'Go away we don't like you.' Not, 'Stick around and admire the view.'"

She turned to see two boys standing near the school entrance. The one who'd spoken, who was now grinning at her, was Eli Brennington. Even though she'd never met him, almost everyone on the island could recognize the Brennington's only son. The other boy she didn't know, but she didn't care, either. She wasn't in the mood for conversation or introductions.

"Eli, enough," the other boy said, before Cassie could tell them in the rudest way possible to leave her alone. "We didn't think you'd still be here, but we came out to check as soon as they released us. That, in there, *sucked*. I couldn't wait to hear your dad's speech, and then, I can't believe that happened. I've never hated this place more."

Cassie folded her arms across her chest. "Well, that makes two of us."

The boy stepped forward, holding out his hand. "I'm Ronan. Ronan Saunders. So, is your dad still here? I really hoped I'd get the chance to meet him. I've heard so much about him and everything he's accomplished." He looked around eagerly for Cassie's father.

She glanced at his hand, not taking it. Even though she preferred members of her dad's fan club to those who'd throw things at him, she didn't really want to interact with either group at the moment.

"No, he's not here," she said.

"Your dad left you? What, are you supposed to hitchhike home?" Eli asked, stepping closer to her as if she'd just become more interesting.

She opened her mouth to defend her father, an old habit, especially when the criticism came from a member of the old families, but Eli kept talking before she could get a word in.

"That is *exactly* the kind of thing my dad would do, and actually, come to think of it, he did do that. Last year. Yeah, remember Ronan? He told me later it was a learning experience, so I'd be better prepared to face the real world, or some such rot. The man has three limos. I think the real world is treating him just fine. When was the last time he had to hitchhike anywhere?"

Cassie was a little taken aback. Since—or maybe, despite the fact—that all three families were related, they were famous for their loyalty to each other. She had never heard any of them badmouth a relative in public before. Something in Eli's honesty pulled at her, drawing out honesty of her own. She decided against the lie she'd been about to tell about her dad coming back for her later.

"Yeah, he left," she said. "But it wasn't to teach me a lesson. He's not like that. He wouldn't do that. He just...he forgot about me, I guess." Cassie couldn't help but wish her dad had done it as a lesson, because at least then, it would have meant he recalled her existence.

"That must have been a rough thing for him to go through," Ronan said. "I'm sure he'll remember soon and be back for you."

"Or not. Who knows?" Eli said lightly. "Either way, why waste time out here when we're officially on holiday? Come on, you might as well get a personalized tour of the Academy, complete with dining hall ice cream and hiding from all the professors who have a different definition of *area off-limits* than we do."

Cassie smiled despite herself, but then she looked warily back at the building.

"Everyone in there hates me," she said.

"Well the front of this school is about to be flooded with students and their parents," Ronan said. "So if your plan is to avoid as many people as possible, you might have better luck with us."

"Besides," Eli added. "Ronan's the only new luminator in our class. I'm the sole person who likes him here, so you'll be in good company."

She glanced back and forth between the two boys in front of her, her curiosity piqued in spite of herself. "Why are you two friends? It's not like you can have much in common."

Ronan was about to answer when Eli stopped him. "Maybe we'll tell you on the tour," Eli said.

Cassie almost said no, but then she imagined her dad coming back to the school in an hour, frantic that he'd forgotten her, only to find the front of the school deserted. There was a part of her that relished the idea of him running through the halls, searching the rooms, desperate to find her. She said yes, and three hours later, she realized that she'd stumbled onto friendship. When Ronan's parents came to pick him up for the long weekend, and her father was still nowhere to be found, they drove her back home. For the first time, when she walked back into her deserted house, Cassie hadn't felt quite so alone.

"I GOT AN APPRENTICESHIP," Ronan said, his words pulling Cassie abruptly out of her reverie.

"What? Seriously?" she asked, turning around suddenly and making Eli run right into her.

"Oomph. Watch where you're going, woman," Eli said.

"You ran into me," Cassie retorted.

"Because you *stopped—*"

"That's so great, Ronan," she said, cutting Eli off. "Who's it with?"

Cassie tried to infuse as much enthusiasm as she could into her voice. She was happy for Ronan, of course. She knew how much he wanted an apprenticeship, but there was always part of her that resisted talk of lumination. If the topic came up in conversation for too long, she would start to feel a strange weighted sensation building in her chest, as if she were being slowly buried under the words. Though she never shared her feelings with anyone, deep down, Cassie resented the trade for taking so much of her father, and in turn, her life.

"Well, I kind of had two offers," Ronan answered her. "One with Andrew Angler, but the Council nixed that one. Then—"

"They took away your apprenticeship?" Eli interrupted, his forehead creasing. "How?"

Ronan shrugged. "They said Angler hadn't kept up with his licensing fees. But I have a feeling it was more likely that someone rich and powerful bribed someone...not so rich and powerful."

"Sounds like my relatives," Eli said lightly, though Cassie thought she heard some bitterness in his tone.

"Yeah, so anyways, then I got another invitation...from Ben Roscoe."

No one said anything for a minute.

"Talk about the black sheep of the family," Eli said. "Does he even practice anymore? I thought he was crazy...and you know, hated everyone. No one ever mentions him around our house."

"It's not like I have people knocking down my door begging to train me," Ronan said, a bit defensively. "I have to take what I can get."

"Actually I did hear something about him a while ago. My cousin told me that Ben threw a client out a window one time," Eli said.

"I'm sure the rumors make him seem worse than he is," Cassie said with a warning look at Eli.

"I'll find out the day after tomorrow," Ronan said.

"He was really good once, right?" she asked. "So what if he's a little...off now. At least he knows what he's doing."

"Or he used to," Eli said, his voice rising theatrically. "And now, he can tell his mind is fading, and he wants to take one bright young kid down with him as he totally loses it."

"Thanks for that, Eli. You always help me look on the bright side of things," Ronan said.

"Just want to prepare you for all possible outcomes."

"I'll give you a bright side," Cassie said, sweeping a low-hanging branch out of the pathway. "Maybe you'll find out what really happened to him."

Ronan shrugged. "I'd rather get my full license."

"Multi-tasking, my friend," she replied.

"We'll see. Hey, back at my house, you said something about this summer being special. Why's that?" Ronan asked.

"Finally," Cassie said, throwing up her hands. "I said that to both of you, and it still took forever for one of you to ask about it."

"I don't think you told me that," Eli said.

"Yes, I did, but you weren't listening."

"In my defense, you talk a lot. One can only pay attention to so many words, so –"

"Anyways," Ronan interrupted. "Summer. Special. Why?"

"Adele's here!" Cassie announced, bouncing with excitement. "It was this crazy, last-minute thing. Her mum called my dad a few days ago and asked if she could spend the entire summer with us."

"Who's Adele?" Eli asked, and then ducked Cassie's half-hearted punch in his direction.

For years before she'd known Eli and Ronan, Cassie considered Adele her only real friend. As much as she loved the guys, she and Adele had a unique flavor of friendship, stemming from years of shared memories. Their moms had met at university on the Scottish mainland, and they stayed close after graduation even though Cassie's mum moved back to Islayne, and Adele's mum stayed in Scotland. After Cassie's mother died, Adele and her mother started coming to the island twice a year to visit, and they were still doing that now over eleven years later.

The guys had only met Adele once, three years ago, right around the time Cassie had started to become friends with them. Adele and her mum always came in the spring and fall, during Adele's school breaks, when Ronan and Eli were in their busiest time at the Academy, so this would be the first time they had seen her in years. Cassie was ecstatic. She already had about a year's worth of things planned for the four of them to do over the next few months.

"So...where is she?" Eli asked.

"I dropped her off at the top with the stuff," Cassie said, gesturing vaguely upward as they started to climb the steeper slope. "So I could come get you guys."

"You left her alone in the middle of the night on a deserted part of the island?" Eli asked. "I'm sure that was a great welcome for her."

Cassie shrugged. "She's fine. Someone had to watch the stuff."

"If we'd just driven in the first place," Eli muttered. "Then the stuff could have stayed in your car."

Cassie pretended not to hear him. Finally, they reached the crest of the hill and the clearing where the lane broke up into many different trails. If it had been during the day, Cassie would have made them stop to take in the sweeping views of the island that could be seen from this spot. She made this trek a few times a month just to look out at the vibrant green sloping hills, dotted with farmsteads, and the steep, sudden drop of the cliffs, leading to the turbulent blue waters far below. But since it was midnight, she walked right past the clearing and chose a hiking path farthest to the left, leading them into more woods. After twenty more minutes of walking, they stepped out of the woods to see a large lake.

"Finally!" Cassie exclaimed. "That seemed to take so much longer the second time around."

She waved to Adele sitting on the beach. In her excitement, Cassie almost missed Ronan's look of shock as he caught sight of Adele's face.

4

Ronan heard the far-off roar of rushing water, but he couldn't place where the sound was coming from. Then he forgot all about the noise when he saw who was waiting for them by the shoreline. About a hundred feet ahead, a figure sat next to two large double kayaks. Ronan could clearly see her curly brown hair in the moonlight. He slowed down and let Cassie and Eli walk ahead of him. It was the girl from the bookstore.

"Oh good, no Viking ghost took you captive," Cassie said as she pulled Adele to her feet.

"Wouldn't that be the Valkyries' job?" Adele asked.

"No, no, the Valkyries picked out which Vikings were going to die in battle, and then spirited them away to Odin's palace, and then became their waitresses—big time demotion, if you ask me."

Adele caught sight of Ronan as he walked up behind Cassie and Eli. He thought he saw her eyes widen in surprise for a moment, but then she went on talking to Cassie.

"Uh, I don't know. I think it'd depend on the tips. So, are you going to introduce me or just keep impressing everyone with how much you know about Norse mythology?"

"You met them a few years ago, remember? Adele, Eli and Ronan. Eli and Ronan, Adele. There. Re-introductions made. Now, let's get to it."

"Nice to re-meet you guys," Adele said, not showing the slightest sign of recognition when she looked at Ronan a second time.

Why was she pretending that they hadn't had a whole conversation just a few days ago? Ronan wasn't sure what he'd been expecting when she saw him, but it wasn't politeness. He thought she would at least yell, or demand that he leave, or throw something to get back at him for dropping a book on her foot. It bothered him that she barely seemed to register his existence. Sure, he made a terrible impression the other day, but if anything, it wasn't forgettable. Why wasn't she bringing it up now?

Before he could think more about it, Ronan suddenly realized where they were and what Cassie had planned for tonight. He'd never been here in the middle of the night before, which was why it had taken him a minute to recognize Tudic Lake. Known for being one of the most dangerous bodies of water on the island, the turbulent lake bordered a cliff at its northernmost tip, and the water spilled over into a breath-taking, deadly waterfall. Multiple rivers fed into the lake, creating strong and unpredictable currents that could pull unsuspecting swimmers or kayakers toward the sharp rocks and rapids on the northern side, or—in the worst cases—push them over the cliff's edge. Though the southern part of the lake closer to the woods was normally more serene, with enough rainfall, even the placid water could hide stronger currents underneath the surface.

Of course, because of that fact, some of the more adventurous islanders and tourists had made a game of racing toward the cliff side of the lake, playing a version of chicken to see who would bow out first and steer their vessel toward the shore. But even those people didn't do it at night. Stupidity had its limits for most of humanity, though apparently not for Cassie.

"Cass, we are not doing this right now," Ronan said to her. "Do you have any idea how dangerous this could be?"

"Relax, Ronan. People do this all the time."

"Actually no, people only do this during the day. And even those people are idiots."

"You're making too big of a deal about this," Cassie said. "It's like racing in a big pool. We'll be fine!"

"Really? Know of any pools with insanely strong currents that can dash your kayak against sharp rocks or push you over the edge of a waterfall?"

"Remember what I said about facing your fears?" Cassie asked, starting to push one of the kayaks toward the water.

"This is different," Ronan said, stepping forward and catching the kayak before she could shove it any further. "People have died doing this."

"Is he right, Cassie?" Adele asked.

Cassie glared at Ronan. "Okay, yes, there may have been a few accidents a long time ago. But that was different. We've kayaked before! We're not amateurs."

"That is the very definition of what we are! And I'd prefer to stay a living one," Ronan said.

"Yeah, I don't know about this," Adele added.

Cassie gave Ronan another death glare and inclined her head slightly in Adele's direction. He knew that she was trying to tell him that she was doing this for Adele, but Ronan didn't care. He glared back at her. Cassie failed to realize that Adele's hypothetical good time would be cut short by all of their cold and watery deaths.

Ronan looked to Eli for support, but Eli wouldn't meet his gaze. That was typical. He would argue with Cassie all day long, but once she decided to do something, he never stood in her way. They all waited in silence for a moment, and he could see Cassie internally debating what to do.

"Okay, fine," she said. "How about this? We don't go near the north side. We won't race toward the cliff. We can just stay around here. No one has ever died from kayaking around the southern part of the lake."

Ronan considered her compromise. As long as they stayed far enough away from the cliff, then they should avoid the strong currents. It was still a risk, but he knew Cassie was giving up a lot by her concession. He looked out over the lake; the water undulated like rippling black velvet in the darkness. He'd never kayaked at night before. He wanted to experience this new side of the island.

"Okay," Ronan said. "As long as we stay away from the cliff, I'm in."

"Yes!" Cassie said. "Adele?"

She nodded.

"Great! Eli and I can take this one. You ride with Ronan. Rescue him if he falls in."

Cassie and Eli got into the first kayak and pushed it out into the water.

"Why do I have the feeling you would very much not rescue me if I fell in?" Ronan asked Adele after Cassie was out of earshot.

"I would, for Cassie. But only after I left you in the water for a few minutes. My foot still hurts, you know."

"So you do remember me," Ronan said as they both dragged the other kayak toward the lake. "Why didn't you say anything?"

"How about we make a deal?" Adele asked. "You won't tell Cass how I acted, and I won't tell her that you assaulted me."

"That's an exaggeration."

"Those books were heavy!"

"Thus why I accidentally dropped them."

"Threw them. At me."

"Shh, the trauma must have affected your memory."

She laughed at that, but just for a second, as if the sound escaped her by accident. Ronan felt something catch in his chest at the sound of it. She had a beautiful laugh.

They were out on the water now, Adele in the front of the kayak and Ronan in the back, with Cassie and Eli in the midst of another argument a few yards away from them. Ronan and Adele paddled far enough away from their friends to be out of earshot of their raised voices. Ronan could just barely make out the soft sound of the water lapping up against the shoreline. The surface of the lake looked denser and richer in the darkness, and Ronan could see the moon's distorted reflection rippling in the distance. They both paddled in silence for a few minutes.

"I am sorry about earlier—at the bookstore," he said finally. "I'm not normally that much of an ass. You caught me at a really bad time."

"I wasn't exactly on my best behavior either," she said. "I guess we can call it even."

"So, why don't you want Cassie to know you were upset?" Ronan asked.

"Why do you like to ask strangers personal questions?"

"I figure we're not going to be strangers much longer. Cassie has plans for the four of us to spend the entire summer together. We might as well get to know each other. And I'm trying to show you that I'm not usually the insensitive jerk that I was the other day. Is it working?"

Adele cocked her head to the side, as if considering his words. She was silent for so long, staring out over the water, that Ronan thought she wasn't going to answer him at all.

"Cassie's actually older than I am, by a few months," she said finally. "But the way she gets excited about things, she's like a little kid. She was so happy when she found out I'd be coming for the whole summer, so it's just easier if she doesn't know the real reason I'm down here, and that I'm not happy about it. Once she got over her disappointment, she'd want to talk it to death, to figure out a solution. It's better for everyone if she doesn't know yet. I kinda wish I could forget myself."

"Forgetting isn't better," Ronan said automatically, the repeated mantras at the Academy flooding his mind. *Memories are sacred. Memories make us human.* "Well, at least I sure hope not," he added in a lighter tone, realizing how abrupt he'd sounded. "Otherwise I'll never be able to make a living."

Adele glanced back at him warily. "That's right. You're one of those luminators. I have to say I think forgetting might exist for a reason. If it wasn't for Cassie's dad, I'd still be super freaked out by you people. As it is, I still think what you can do is...creepy."

"You can't be serious," Ronan said.

"Of course I'm serious! If you wanted to right now, you could pull all of my memories out of my head, look at anything you want, and then make me remember any scene as distinctly as if I'd just lived it. Heck, you could find a memory of a nightmare I had when I was seven, and then boom, there it would be in my mind, clear as day. You could really mess some people up if you wanted to."

Ronan could feel the blood start to pound in his ears. Of all the small-minded, stupid things to think. How could someone as seemingly intelligent and normal as Adele know so little about how the trade worked and believe the most ridiculous ideas?

"Have you ever read anything about lumination, the history of Islayne, or the regulations of the Council?" Ronan asked, not trying to mask his derision. "I couldn't do it here, because we're way outside of the borders of the Lumin District. My powers wouldn't work. Besides that, the only buildings large enough to contain the memories during a session are the luminator offices or maybe one or two of the old families' mansions in the Lumin District. Neither of which I could just sneak into easily, and I couldn't do a session out in the open. It's much harder to contain memories when you aren't in an enclosed space, and memories produce *noise*. A pretty distinct, loud hum. If I tried to complete an illegal session with you outside, do you know how quickly a Council enforcer would find me and put an end to it? And then do you know how quickly I'd be found guilty before a tribunal, kicked off Islayne, and be forced to watch my gifting fade out?"

She turned around again. Was she fighting a smile? Ronan couldn't tell for sure in the moonlight, but the thought only made him more frustrated. This wasn't a joke. This mattered. She was about to say something else, but Ronan was too angry to let her get a word in.

"But even if we didn't have these and about a dozen other safeguards in place—which, you know, aren't that hard to find out about, considering they've been around ever since the old families opened the trade to the public—I would *never* use my gifting against a client's will, especially not just to satisfy my own curiosity! People come here to understand their own lives better. What luminators discover in session is held in the strictest confidence. The memories are for our clients, not for us. And besides, I doubt your memories would be worth the effort."

Those last words wiped the hint of a smile off Adele's face, and even in the poor lighting, Ronan could see the hurt in her eyes. The anger deflated a bit in his chest.

"Oh no! You did it already?" Cassie asked. "I heard the shouting and came right over. Did he cry? Insult your family? Try to push you into the lake?"

Ronan jumped at the proximity of Cassie's voice. He hadn't noticed his friends coming back over to their kayak.

"What are you talking about?" Ronan asked, glancing back and forth between Cassie and Adele.

"I told Adele she should tell you that she was freaked out by luminators," Cassie said. "And then sit back and watch the show."

"You what? Wait, you don't really think those things?" Ronan directed the question at Adele. She stared at him for a moment, cool and collected again, and then ignored him and turned to Cassie.

"He might have gotten to tears if it had gone on much longer. But no, so far it had only been contempt, shouting, and insults. Not too shabby," she said.

Ronan's guilt over what he'd said was quickly being replaced by annoyance.

"I'm glad you two find me so entertaining," he said.

"Oh don't sulk, Ronan. It was just a joke," Cassie said.

"For what it's worth," Eli chimed in. "I find your shouting grating and your insults unoriginal, so I didn't think it was very entertaining at all."

"Anyways, now that we've wrung all the amusement we can out of this, we're off again," Cassie said, pointing out across the water theatrically. She and Eli paddled away.

Ronan and Adele sat in strained silence for a moment. Or at least, it seemed strained to Ronan. He had no idea what Adele was feeling.

"A small part of me wants to apologize for doing that to you," she finally said. "But then you were kind of an ass again, so I'm not going to."

"Well, you were a jerk to make me believe you thought that about me, about luminators. So, I'm not going to apologize either."

"Why does it matter so much to you? What people think about the trade?"

Ronan hesitated. The truth was, it normally didn't matter that much to him. While it was rarer by this point to find people who thought luminators were evil or creepy, they did still exist. Ronan knew that, and he didn't lose sleep over it. But for some reason, he cared what Adele thought of him.

Which didn't make any sense.

"Public opinion affects the trade's bottom line," he said, and then mentally kicked himself for coming up with the lamest reason ever.

She threw her head back and laughed. "Oh my God, you sound like a middle-aged accountant."

"Well, that *is* my backup career choice," he replied, happy to hear her laugh again.

"Good to know I'll have someone to do my taxes at a discount down the road."

"Who said you'd get special treatment?" he asked. "After that stunt you pulled, I'd charge you double my rate."

"In five years, you'll still be nursing this grudge?" she asked.

"I can be quite tenacious."

"That's a nice way to say pig-headed."

Ronan could feel something loosening in his chest as they kept talking. By the time Adele finished telling him about how she and Cassie had once convinced Cassie's neighbor, Mrs. Peabody, that her shed was haunted, any last trace of his earlier irritation had vanished. He realized he'd been missing out on something all these years, not ever spending time with Adele during her visits to Islayne. He felt a surge of gratitude toward Cassie for her militant plans for the four of them to spend the summer together. The coming months felt suddenly rife with opportunity for more evenings like this one. Ronan grinned in the moonlight.

Just then, Cassie yelled out his name across the water. He and Adele turned to see the other kayak heading toward the northern tip of the lake. For a moment, he thought his friends had been caught in one of currents, but then he heard Cassie laughing, and he realized they were paddling toward the cliff on purpose. He should have known she'd try to force him to race, and he should have known Eli would agree to it.

"Cassie!" Ronan shouted. "Stop being an idiot. Slow down!"

"There's only one way to make that happen, Ronan!" she called back over her shoulder.

"Oh my God," Adele said, a note of panic rising in her voice. "What is she doing? She promised!"

"You can yell at her for it sometime when her life's not in danger," Ronan said, changing the direction of their kayak.

They both began paddling as fast as they could, and they slowly started to gain on Cassie and Eli. As they neared the northern edge of the lake, Ronan could hear the roar of the waterfall below, and he could just make out the vicious white rapids in the moonlight. He remembered watching the news story of the tourist who died here a few years ago; later he looked it up online, and he could still recall the images of the man's battered, bruised body laid out by the shoreline. Ronan pushed those thoughts away. He and Adele were gaining on the other kayak, and in a few moments, they would be able to cut Eli and Cassie off and make them turn around. Other than Cassie pouting over him ruining her fun, nothing bad would happen tonight.

Suddenly, Cassie's scream pierced through the other nighttime noises.

5

IN THE MOONLIGHT, RONAN SAW HIS FRIENDS' KAYAK HEADING STRAIGHT FOR one of the massive rocks. Both Eli and Cassie tried to steer it away, but the current was too strong. The kayak rammed into the stone and flipped over. A few agonizingly slow seconds passed as Ronan stared at the ominous smooth underside of the vessel, still too far away to do anything. Then the kayak righted, but only Eli was still inside, coughing and sputtering. Ronan saw Cassie pop out of the water next, about twenty feet away from Eli. The rough current began to force her closer and closer to the edge of the cliff.

Ronan changed directions again and began to steer the kayak toward the shoreline nearest to the cliff.

"What are you doing?" Adele cried. "You have to help them!"

"That's what I'm trying to do!" he yelled back. "If we go straight towards them, we'll just get caught in the same current. We need to get back to the shore and head for the cliff on foot. We should be able to get pretty close, and the opening isn't that wide, so hopefully we can drag her back onto land."

After a minute of hard rowing, they reached the shoreline. Ronan didn't even think about dragging the kayak up onto dry land. As soon as it was shallow enough, he and Adele jumped out and started running. He kept his paddle so they wouldn't have to waste time finding something else for

Cassie to hold. They didn't speak. Ronan couldn't hear anything except the sound of his labored breathing. It was as if the rest of the island had ceased to exist. There was only Cassie speeding toward the cliff, and too much ground between them and her.

She's going too fast, he thought, beginning to panic. *We're not going to get there in time.* Ronan saw Cassie desperately trying to grasp on to anything, but the rocks were too slippery. She had managed to get closer to the shoreline, but it wouldn't matter if she didn't slow down. Ronan knew he and Adele wouldn't reach the edge for at least another five minutes.

Just then, Ronan saw Eli steering his kayak into the worst of the rapids. Ronan had no idea how he had gained ground so quickly paddling by himself, or how he'd kept the kayak from flipping again, but somehow, he'd managed to get just ahead of Cassie. Then he turned the kayak sharply and wedged it in between two smaller rocks, directly in Cassie's path. Ronan feared that she would be shoved under the kayak by the force of the current, but as she neared Eli, he reached out his paddle, and she grabbed hold of it. He slowly pulled it toward him, and then grabbed her arm and dragged her onto the kayak.

Ronan willed his legs to go faster. Eli had bought them the time they needed, but Ronan knew that the kayak wouldn't last long where it was. He could already see the force of the current making it wobble; soon, the rushing water would push the kayak out from where it was wedged. His friends had little time before they'd be thrown over the edge, and they still looked impossibly far away.

Ronan's lungs started to burn as they kept running, the paddle began to feel heavier and more cumbersome in his hands, and his legs seemed to be filling up with lead. *Hold on,* he thought. *Please hold on.* Finally, after what felt like forever, he and Adele reached the edge of the water near the drop off.

There was a large boulder a few feet above Cassie and Eli. Ronan scrambled onto it, but the surface was much slicker than he had anticipated. His foot slipped, and Ronan's knees hit the boulder hard. The paddle almost fell out of his grip as he fought to keep his balance. Ronan teetered close to the water's edge, the spray from the rapids drenching his face. Then Adele reached out and grabbed his arm, pulling him back and helping him regain his balance. His eyes met hers for the briefest of moments before she released her grip.

Ronan braced himself against the boulder and extended the paddle out into the foaming water. Cassie, though clearly exhausted and battered from the rough currents, reached out and grabbed hold of it. Slowly, she pulled herself toward them, hand over hand, until she was close enough for Adele to grab her under her arms and drag her the rest of the way up onto the boulder. Cassie was coughing and shaking from the cold water, but she was alive. She crawled back toward the land.

Ronan turned back to Eli and extended the paddle again. Eli reached for it, but he missed. The kayak shuddered under his shifting weight, and Eli's eyes widened in fear as he fought to keep his balance. The roar of the waterfall filled Ronan's ears as he reached the paddle out farther, and this time Eli grasped it with both hands and began to pull himself toward the rock. Ronan watched intently as his friend slowly put one hand in front of the other, as if the force of Ronan's concentration could keep Eli's grasp from slipping. Finally, he reached the boulder. Once Adele had a firm grip on Eli's arms, Ronan dropped the paddle, and they both pulled him to safety. Ronan heard a scraping sound and looked back just as the current wrenched the kayak out from between the two rocks. The vessel careened out into the foaming water, and a moment later, disappeared over the edge of the waterfall.

All four of them collapsed on the nearby grass without saying anything, trying to catch their breath. Eli and Cassie shivered from their wet clothes in the cool nighttime air.

"Not too bad for being out of practice." Cassie finally broke the silence.

Ronan opened his mouth to reply, but Adele beat him to it.

"What the hell, Cass?!" she shouted. "What is wrong with you? You promised not to race! Do you have some kind of death wish?"

The teasing smile vanished from Cassie's face. "I just wanted to do something exciting to start off the summer."

"Sure, yeah, watching you drown right in front of my eyes. That would be a fantastic way to start a holiday."

"It would be memorable," Cassie said in a small voice.

"Stop trying to be funny. Your *life* is not a joke. Do you have any idea how scared I was?! And for what? So you could have a good time?"

"Okay, okay, I'm sorry," Cassie conceded, holding up her hands. "It was a stupid idea."

Adele dug her fingers into the ground, ripping out fistfuls of grass and tossing them away. She stood up abruptly. In the moonlight, Ronan could see the flush in her cheeks and the fire in her eyes; he couldn't help but think that she looked even prettier when she was angry. "I'm going back to the car," she said.

"Yeah, we probably should," Cassie agreed, starting to get up.

"No, I don't want you coming with me. You can leave in a few minutes. I need to be away from you until I stop being so pissed off."

"But, you don't know the way back to Ronan's house," Cassie said hesitantly.

"Oh, do you think that's unsafe? Perfect! Now you can know what it's like to worry about someone else being in danger!" Adele grabbed her flashlight and stormed off.

Cassie hugged her arms tightly against the cold. "I need to go make sure she doesn't get lost. Thanks for saving me from a watery grave, both of you."

Ronan rolled his eyes. "All in a day's work, hanging out with you."

She grinned slightly and then started to walk back to the woods.

"I can't believe I let you talk me into doing that," Eli said quietly.

She sighed and turned around. "I said I'm sorry. It was a dumb idea. I won't do it again."

"You don't sound sorry," Eli muttered.

She hesitated for a moment, as if debating whether or not to argue with him, but then she glanced toward the trail that Adele had taken.

"I *am* sorry," she said. "But I really need to catch up with Adele before she gets lost. We'll talk later." She headed for the forest.

"This is shaping up to be a great summer," Eli said as he watched Cassie walk away.

"Just like always," Ronan replied.

6

Two days later, Ronan raised his hand to knock on Ben's office door, and then lowered it again. He quickly glanced at all the windows at the front of the building. None of the glass panes looked like they had been replaced recently, so Eli's remark about Ben throwing a client out a window was almost definitely a rumor. Almost definitely. *Stop being a coward,* he thought. *You managed to rescue your friends from the edge of a waterfall. You can knock on a recluse's door.*

Ronan's stomach flipped over. He wasn't sure what fifteen years of social isolation would do to a person, but he didn't think it would be good. *This is my only shot,* he reminded himself. And besides, whatever the intervening years had done to the man, at one time, Ben Roscoe had been one of the best luminators on the island, and twice he actually reached the very top of the yearly rankings. Though he had been the darling of his family, no one could attribute his success solely to that advantage. He had excelled in the trade.

And then, seemingly overnight, everything changed. One morning, the newspaper headlines read that Ben Roscoe had publicly cut all ties with his family. He moved out of the Roscoe estate, and no one was exactly sure where he lived afterward, though it had to be somewhere in the Lumin District, since he continued to practice. As both he and his family refused to explain the sudden change, the rumors swelled in the midst of their silence. Ben had squandered the family fortune; Ben's father, Frederick, was abusive and drove him away; Ben's mother, Diane, was having an affair and Ben found out about it. But none of these stories gained any real traction, and after months of the family's silence, the media gave up trying to uncover the truth.

As far as anyone knew, Ben never made any attempt to contact his family or to establish any new connections in the luminator world. In the years following, no one would see him for months at a time. When other islanders did have a chance encounter with him, they would all say the same thing—the more time Ben spent alone, the stranger he seemed to become. Ronan comforted himself with the fact whatever the man's eccentricities, they had never been extreme enough to make him forfeit his practicing license. Ben kept this office rented at the very edge of the Lumin District. Every so often—it seemed just often enough so that his gifting didn't fade out—Ben would take on a client, practice there for a few weeks to a few months, and then close it up again.

Ronan wondered, not for the first time, what would happen if Ben kept up this schedule with Ronan as his apprentice. It would take Ronan forever to clock enough practice hours, and technically, it was against the Council codes. He feared it would be another way the old families would try to invalidate this apprenticeship too.

But that question was overshadowed by a much greater one. Ben had never taken on an apprentice before now. *Why did he pick me?* Ronan thought. *What does he want? Is this all some sort of joke?*

The door swung open.

"You're late. How long have you been standing there?" Ben asked, leaning back against the doorframe and peering doubtfully at Ronan. He looked perfectly normal. In fact, he looked...cool. Like he could be the young owner of some startup tech company in California. He wore fitted jeans, a plain white t-shirt, and a sports coat. Ronan would have guessed that Ben was maybe five years older than himself, though he knew that the man had to be at least in his late thirties. With short brown hair and open features, Ben looked almost exactly like he had in the newspaper stories from fifteen years ago.

Since he looked so young, Ronan was glad he didn't have to think about whether he should call him Ben or Mr. Roscoe. All luminators were called by their first name, unless they taught at the Academy. It was one of the customs the old families put in place back before Ronan was born. They thought it would help clients feel safer and more comfortable if they were on a first-name basis with the person who would be sifting through their private memories.

Ronan realized that he had been staring at Ben for seconds without responding. "Uh, not long," he stammered. "I just got here. Sorry. The drive took longer than I thought."

"Did you cheat at the Academy to get those high marks?" Ben asked.

"What? No!" Ronan said, taken aback. "Of course not."

"Hmm, pity. I was hoping you could tell me how you managed it. Those Academy pricks wouldn't have made it easy. I wanted to see how smart you were."

"Don't you think the fact I didn't cheat and did well might show you how smart I am?" Ronan asked hesitantly.

Ben shrugged. "A more conventional kind of intelligence, I suppose. Well, this has already proved to be less entertaining than I'd hoped."

"Is that why you offered to train me? To be entertained?" Ronan asked.

"Oh no," Ben said, finally stepping back and letting Ronan walk inside. "I wanted you here for this." He gestured around the office.

From his time at the Academy, Ronan knew that every luminator space was designed similarly. There were two small rooms at the front, an office to house paperwork and normally the luminator when not with a client, and the parlor, which would have a few comfortable chairs, a fireplace, and a small kitchenette with tea and light refreshments. Here, the luminator would work with the client to iron out the details of the particular service. He would make sure the client understood exactly what was going to happen and grasped the risks of the procedure.

Once all of the preliminary work was completed, they would move back to the workroom. This was a huge, cavernous space, large enough for the luminator to spread out and organize the memories as needed. It normally spanned about a hundred feet across and stretched up to three stories high, ending in a massive domed ceiling. While the offices were mostly hidden and the parlors were meant to put the client at ease, the workrooms were designed to awe.

But here, the rooms didn't accomplish any of these things. Everywhere Ronan looked there was dust and trash. Random stacks of paper littered the floor, mixed in with half-empty take out containers and plastic cups. The air felt stale and heavy, and the smell of partially-rotting food and old coffee was enough to turn Ronan's stomach.

"Do you *live* here?" Ronan asked, seeing a dilapidated pillow and blanket thrown haphazardly over one of the parlor recliners and a large pile of clothes covering the other.

Ben ignored the question. "Clients were starting to complain about the state of the office," he said, propping his feet up on the coffee table and opening a newspaper. "So, I decided to do something about it."

"Is this why you made me get here so early?" Ronan asked, taking in the mess.

"Now you're putting that conventional intelligence to use," Ben said.

Ronan picked his way carefully through the trash, trying his best not to step on any leftover food, and opened the door to the workroom. Immediately, he heard the faint humming sound that every workroom emanated—the only mark that memories left on a space once a session was completed. The area didn't look as trashed out as the parlor, though he could see client folders stacked haphazardly across the back wall, and a thick layer of dust coated everything. He shut the door and turned back to Ben.

"The Council has rules against using apprentices for this kind of thing, you know," Ronan said.

"Hmm, so report me," Ben murmured, not bothering to look up from the paper. "You can just accept one of your other offers...oh, wait."

Ronan walked closer to him. "That newspaper is from last year," he said.

"Yes, well, I haven't always had an apprentice to do my work for me, so I'm just getting around to it. Now hurry up, you only have a few hours." Ben held out a roll of plastic garbage bags to Ronan, still not moving his eyes from the paper.

On the one hand, Ronan felt relieved that Ben was acting semi-normal. He wasn't arguing with invisible people or yelling at Ronan about the coming apocalypse. But on the other hand, Ronan had tried to prepare himself for crazy. He hadn't planned on his trainer being an arrogant prick and using him for manual labor. A part of Ronan wanted to throw the roll of garbage bags at Ben's smug face and leave. But he couldn't help but wonder if Ben was just testing him to see how much he really wanted this and how much he was willing to work for it. This chance was worth a few hours of chores.

"You know, it would've been a lot cheaper for you to just hire a cleaning service," Ronan said as he tore off one of the bags, shook it out, and started dumping the takeout containers into it. Luminators had to pay the Council a steep fee before they could be approved to train an apprentice.

Ben looked at him sardonically. "Oh, but then I wouldn't have the joy of giving back to the luminator community, investing in the future of the trade, etcetera, etcetera."

Ronan spent the next two hours picking up trash, piling the laundry in the cupboard, opening up all the windows, dusting off the furniture, sweeping, and filing the old client folders. Just a few minutes into his work, Ben tossed the paper aside.

"When was the trade first opened to the public?" he asked Ronan abruptly.

"What?" Ronan asked, startled. "Oh, um, 1890. Right? Or 1892?"

"Why did the old families make the change?" Ben continued with no hint as to whether Ronan had answered correctly.

"Why are you asking?"

Ben raised his eyebrows. "Perhaps I'm putting that conventional intelligence to the test and trying to determine whether you're worth my time. So far, it doesn't look promising."

Ronan paused, considering the question. The official answer was that the old families decided it was time to let the wider world benefit from their gifting; the real answer was money. For generations, the old families gained wealth and power by making their talents readily available to whomever controlled the island at the time—first the Vikings, then the King of Norway, then the various Lords of the Isles, down to the Campbells. They were used to amuse guests, interrogate criminals, and empower the mind of the ruler. But by the turn of the last century, the owners of Islayne were much poorer and less interested in the services of the old families. Scrambling to keep themselves financially afloat, they took out a massive loan to create the Academy, build a few offices, and begin to attract clients from abroad, in essence turning lumination into a selective profession.

Ronan guessed that Ben would prefer the latter answer.

"They didn't want to go bankrupt," he answered.

He thought he saw the ghost of a smile on the man's face, but then it was gone again.

"Do you think the way they went about it was wise?"

Ronan paused again. He knew that Ben wasn't exactly close to his family, but Ronan still didn't know how honestly he should answer the question. Ronan thought the families had been foolish to spend so much money all at once, and to put up their land as collateral. They must have thought that clients would start rolling in immediately, and they wouldn't have any trouble paying the bank back in time. They'd been wrong. It took the general public quite a while to overcome their disbelief and fear of the luminator gifting.

He was happy with the results of their shortsightedness, though.

"It may not have been the best business decision they ever made," Ronan said carefully. "But you won't find me complaining about it."

"How did they legitimize the trade to the world?" Ben asked next, his face impassive.

Ronan started to relax. If this was the way Ben wanted to assess his intelligence, then he could handle it. He'd paid close attention at the Academy, and he was good at tests. "They established the Council to regulate the trade and the Academy to teach it accurately. And for years, they invited anyone to come to Islayne and have five free sessions, and soon enough, word spread."

"Who was the top-ranked luminator the first year the Council implemented the ranking system?"

Ronan opened his mouth to respond and then froze. He couldn't remember. He thought back to his class on Council law. Had his professor mentioned that when they talked about rankings? He remembered that the Council started the system in 1910, and of course he knew how it worked. All luminators had to complete a closed memory session before the Council each year. They were scored according to how much control they exhibited over memories, how deftly they sifted through them, and how many scenes they could brighten per session. The rankings were a big deal because the higher the score, the more clients a luminator would receive from the Council, the more they could bill for their services, and the easier it was to keep up with the exorbitant Council fees required to maintain a license.

But none of those details he so easily recalled gave him the answer he needed. So much for a good first impression.

"I don't know," he said. "Oh wait, yes I do! It was your grandfather, wasn't it? Adrian Roscoe?"

Ben grunted and then picked up his newspaper. "I never told you to stop sweeping while you talked," he said as settled back into the chair.

RONAN CONTINUED to clean while Ben remained in the exact same seated position and never turned the pages of his paper. Once Ronan finished wiping down the fireplace mantle in the parlor, he finally gathered his courage to ask the question he'd been wanting to voice all morning.

"Ben?"

The man glanced up from his paper, looking annoyed at the interruption.

Why did you choose now to take on an apprentice? The words stuck in his throat. "Uh, how, how did you know that...my apprenticeship with Andrew Angler was invalidated? I got your note on the same day the Council rescinded my other offer." *Chicken*, a voice inside his mind chided.

"I didn't," Ben responded. "That was a coincidence. I just assumed you wouldn't get any offers."

"Why not?" Ronan asked, feeling the frustration rise inside him.

"Because of all the luminators on this island, I'm the only one with nothing to lose." And then Ben went back to his paper, making it clear that their conversation was over. Ronan had no idea what to make of his answer.

After a full two hours of free child labor, when all three main rooms and the bathroom looked decently clean, Ben told Ronan to come sit across from him in the parlor.

"Her name is Jillian Poe," Ben said, sliding a crisp, new folder across the coffee table to Ronan. "She's coming here to have memories of her late husband revived. Looks like he kicked the bucket a few months back."

Ronan looked up in surprise at Ben's cavalier tone.

"Something to say?" Ben asked.

"You could have a little more compassion for her," Ronan said.

Ben shrugged. "I'm not a counselor. I'm here to give the client what they paid for. Why Jillian wants these memories or what she'll do with them when she has them—that's not my concern. Don't they still teach professional distance at the Academy?"

"Yeah, but it doesn't mean you have to be such a..."

"A dick?"

"Well, I didn't say it."

Ben rolled his eyes. "I couldn't care less if you did say it. Your opinion doesn't hold any weight with me. But my livelihood and my clients' minds do. In this trade, you have to do whatever is necessary to keep your emotions in check until the proper time. Because if you begin a session distracted by sympathy or anger or curiosity, you could end up making a fatal mistake. In Jillian's case, I think she would prefer her sanity to your empathy. Or mine. Are we clear?"

Ronan nodded. So maybe his apprenticeship wasn't a joke to Ben, after all.

"Good. Now start reading. She'll be here in a few minutes."

Ronan thumbed through the folder. It was much thinner than normal.

From his Academy training, Ronan knew that each client folder consisted of a few sheets of contact information, about twenty pages of different liability waivers, and then another dozen pages with specific questions about memories. Clients were encouraged to write about the key memory factor—in Jillian's case, her husband—in as much detail as possible. But in this file, she mostly gave one- or two-word answers to the questions.

Just then, the front doorbell chimed as a tall, graceful woman walked into the office. Ben got up from his chair to greet her. Ronan stood as well, but then he wasn't sure what to do with himself. He gave the woman an awkward smile as Ben ushered her into the parlor. She was at least a head taller than Ronan, with shoulder-length, white blonde hair and very pale skin. From the lines around her eyes and mouth, Ronan guessed that she had to be in her early sixties. She wasn't pretty, per se, but she carried herself with a sort of poise and class that reminded Ronan of royalty. She was the kind of woman who would be at ease in a room full of beautiful, breakable things. It was hard to imagine her cleaning a bathroom or getting cut off in traffic or spilling coffee on her shirt.

"Jillian, thank you for being *right on time*," Ben said with a sideways glance at Ronan. "Please sit down." Ben returned to his chair and gestured for her to sit where Ronan had been seated before. "Ronan, where are the refreshments?"

"What? I don't think that we have any," Ronan said, looking around the parlor.

Ben sighed dramatically. "I asked you to have them ready. My apologies, Jillian. This is his first day. He's still learning."

"Oh, no, that's quite all right," Jillian said, taking a seat. "I don't need anything."

Ronan glared at Ben over the woman's head, and his trainer winked back at him. Ronan sat down in one of the less comfortable chairs a little further back from them. He wasn't sure if he was meant to stay here for this part, but if Ben wanted him to retreat to the office, Ronan was sure he would make his wishes clear.

"Now then, let me tell you a few things about how these sessions will go, and then we will discuss the memory key in detail. I apologize if you've already heard some of this information. We are required by Council law to go over this with all of our clients.

"First, we won't know exactly how many of your memories we can brighten until we are further along in this process, as it will depend on the strength of your mind. Each client's memory is different, and each can contain only a certain number of revived scenes. We'll both be able to tell when we're nearing that breaking point."

Ronan watched Ben closely as he talked. Everything he said was textbook information, and Ronan could only imagine that it would get old giving clients the same speech over and over. But Ben didn't look bored at all. In fact, for the first time all morning, he seemed fully engaged in what he was doing. It was as if a light had switched on somewhere inside of him. Seeing him now, it wasn't hard to imagine Ben dominating the luminator rankings and making headlines with his abilities. This was a man alive. For the first time all morning, Ronan felt a glimmer of admiration for his trainer.

"As I'm sure you already know from filling out the application," Ben continued. "We can't simply revive a whole time period of your life. In your mind, specific memories are centered around what we call a key—the person, or in rarer instances, the place—that was most important to those recollections. Of course, there are one-off memories that don't seem to be connected to anything, but the vast majority of your memories have stuck around because of a significant person or place. In your case, your husband."

"Well, actually, I was wondering if, that is, I want you to find any memories I have of a man named Anthony Ericks," Jillian interjected in a rush. Ronan's head snapped up. That was definitely not the name of her late husband.

"But that's not what's in the folder," he blurted out.

Now it was Ben's turn to glare.

"No, it's not. It's...a bit complicated," Jillian responded. "I couldn't put it on the application. Will that be a problem?"

"No," Ben said. "It's not a problem. Excuse my apprentice for talking out of turn. Like I said, his first day. But we will have to alter the records for the Council."

"But…it won't be put anywhere else? Publicly?" she asked.

"No. We would keep it fully confidential."

She nodded. "I just, well, it's not what you think. I only want to—"

Ben cut her off. "Mrs. Poe, you don't need to justify or explain yourself to us. We are here to work for you."

Ronan knew that Ben was right to stop Jillian from explaining herself—the Academy *did* stress the importance of making the clients feel comfortable and not judged for what memories they hoped to revive. Even so, Ronan couldn't help but wish he had let her explain. If the information in her folder was accurate, she'd been married to her husband for over thirty years. He couldn't imagine this pristine, graceful woman old enough to be his grandmother having an affair. But then again, what did he know? He'd only met her five minutes ago. Only one thing was clear—she hadn't come all this way and spent so much money to relive memories of her dead husband.

"You should try to ready yourself for this experience," Ben continued. "What we revive will be so strong in your mind, it will be as if it occurred yesterday. That is one of the reasons we only brighten a few memories at a time, especially in the beginning. Too many strong memories at once can be overwhelming for a person. Depending on what we uncover, this may be an incredibly emotional time for you. Please let me know if you need to take a longer break between sessions than we have scheduled.

"Now that I've probably bored you to death by talking so much, why don't you take your time and describe Anthony to us? Tell us anything that you can remember—every detail is helpful. Ronan, here, take notes."

Ronan took the pen and paper from Ben's outstretched hand. This was also not part of his job description—every luminator was supposed to have a secretary for this kind of work. But it did beat scrubbing the toilet, so at least he was making progress.

After an hour of furious note taking while Jillian answered Ben's questions about Anthony, Ben explained the potential risks of the sessions, and then said it was time to begin. Jillian stood up, and Ronan could see that her hands were shaking slightly. His trainer assured her that it was perfectly normal to be nervous at this part, but that he'd done this countless times, and she had nothing to worry about. Ronan thought the many pages of liability waivers she'd signed might indicate another story.

Lumination was inherently dangerous; there was no way around it. Once a luminator accessed a client's mind, the memories inside were wild, untamable entities. They had a kind of magnetic force that could draw an untrained luminator in unawares, swallowing him whole, and causing the client to have a complete mental breakdown. It had only happened a few times in the last hundred years, but each case had rocked Islayne to the core. That was one of the reasons why the Council developed very strict rules about the level of training required before apprentices could apply for their full licenses and practice independently.

Ben led Jillian back to the workroom. Ronan heard her small gasp of surprise when she stepped into the giant space. Ben brought her to a long, reclined chair situated in the middle of the floor. At his instructions, she laid back in the chair, closed her eyes, and began taking deep breaths.

He placed his hands on either side of her head. The faint hum in the room grew instantly louder and more distinct. Ronan saw Jillian relax into the chair as Ben lulled her into the dream state, which would ease her mind enough to allow her memories to be drawn out and would also protect her from the memories' pull.

"Okay," Ben said. "Now we'll begin."

Ronan leaned against the back wall of the workroom, where he would be well outside the pullspace, the circular area around the luminator, about ten feet in circumference, in which the magnetic force of the memories could be felt. At the Academy, he'd only been allowed into the space when multiple luminators kept the entirety of the memories' pull from touching him. Ronan assumed that Ben would want him to steer clear of the space until his trainer put him through a few weeks of the typical mind-strengthening exercises to make sure he could handle the memory pull.

Ben glanced over at Ronan. "You won't be able to learn much way over there. Come stand by me."

Ronan gaped at him, sure that he must have misheard. "What?"

"Alright, you caught me. I don't care about you learning, but I do best with an up-close audience."

"But that, I mean, on my first day, you haven't tested me for that yet."

Ben shrugged. "I'll keep most of the memory-pull away from you while I work. As long as you aren't completely inept, you'll be fine."

Ronan stepped into the pullspace. He could feel the hum now, reverberating in his bones, filling up the workroom. In those few, controlled sessions at the Academy, after Ronan had pulled a few memories from a client's mind, he'd had to return to the observatory and watch the real work of lumination occur from behind a thick pane of glass. Those had still been incredible moments, but to be in the center of the pullspace during a session, to see the memories clearly, to hear them, to *feel* them...nothing would compare to this.

He thought it must be like the difference between seeing fireworks light up the sky from miles below, and then suddenly being poised in midair, in the midst of the color, the brilliance, and the flame. Ronan shuddered in anticipation.

He watched his trainer, standing perfectly still, his fingers lightly resting on Jillian's temples. The seconds passed slowly. Ronan wondered briefly why he was taking so long. Then Ben looked sideways at Ronan and smiled.

The room exploded.

7

A LOUD ROAR SUPPLANTED THE STEADY HUM FROM A MOMENT BEFORE, AND light burst forth from the middle of the room. Ronan covered his face and braced himself for flying debris. For a split second, he thought Ben truly was crazy and had somehow detonated a bomb. But as he slowly got his bearings, Ronan realized that his trainer had just skipped a few of the normal steps when starting a session.

A luminator was supposed to draw out a client's memories slowly, allowing them to only gradually flow out of the client's head and up into the space of the workroom. Steadily, the memories would fill the upper reaches of the dome in a complicated network of clusters and strands, called a mindscape, until the ceiling looked like a night sky full of brilliantly-lit constellations. The whole process normally took at least half an hour.

Then, the luminator could focus his mind and pull a specific cluster down closer to him, enlarging it until individual memories hovered in the air, like large raindrops stopped mid-fall. He would sift through these until he could discern the memory key. Because of the powerful force of the mindscape, luminators were supposed to be cautious and deliberate. If one didn't take the time to either let the memories pour forth from the client's mind slowly, or to gradually pull a specific cluster closer, it greatly increased the chance that a memory could overpower and swallow the luminator. The slower one worked, the more control one had over individual memories.

Instead, Ben had forced the mindscape out from Jillian's head in one massive rush, and then he immediately pulled down three different memory clusters at random. The scenes had all begun to play at once, thus the explosion of sound and light. A new fear rose up in Ronan at this realization. Ben must have forgotten how to do this. They could be in serious danger.

But then Ronan saw his trainer's face. He didn't looked panicked at all. In fact, Ben seemed to be completely in control. Suddenly, the roaring noise quieted, and the lights stopped shifting. Ronan couldn't believe what he was seeing. With what looked like barely any mental strain, Ben had managed to silence all of the memories in these clusters at the same time. Ronan stared at his trainer. No one could exert that much mental force against so many memories all at once. No luminator was that powerful.

Ben spent the next hour sorting through more scenes than Ronan would have thought possible. He didn't do it with any of the precision or strategy that Ronan had seen in others. He would draw forth a cluster, freeze the memories, then bring a few close to him seemingly at random. He never spent longer than a minute examining each scene, and soon enough he would push the entire cluster back into the mindscape, choose another one, and repeat the process all over again. Though Ronan could feel the draw of the memories, it was slight. His trainer had to be using an incredible amount of focus to keep so much of the magnetic force of the mindscape from touching Ronan.

Finally, Ben seemed to find one of the memory clusters he was looking for. He turned to Ronan.

"Want to try your hand at brightening the first memory?" Ben asked, not showing any of the strain of the past hour.

Ronan couldn't believe what he'd heard. It was crazy enough that his trainer allowed him to be in the pullspace on his very first day, but to do a solo? There wasn't a law against it, per se, but it was tradition for apprentices to be awarded their first solo session at the start of their third year if they'd proved their talent and dedication in the first two years. Was Ben testing him? Was Ronan supposed to say no? The thing was, reckless though it might be, Ronan desperately wanted to do it. For all he knew, the old families could be figuring out a way to invalidate this apprenticeship as well. If this might be Ronan's only chance to revive a memory, how could he turn that down?

"Yes," he said before he could second-guess himself. Ben looked surprised, but then he nodded and motioned for Ronan to come stand directly in front of the memory. He enlarged it so that the scene was about as tall as Ronan, and twice as wide. Even though he knew that Ben was still holding back most of the magnetic draw, Ronan could now feel much more of the pulsing power emanating from the frozen scene in front of him. He could sense how old and frail this memory was, and still it held such force. Ronan wondered what it would feel like to stand so close to a well-remembered scene.

He took a deep breath and focused on the minutiae of the memory. Through the muted colors and blurred images in front of him, Ronan could barely make out a shorter, stockier man on a path next to a lake. Ronan took a deep breath, reached out with his mind, and began to play the memory. He could faintly hear the wind rustling through the tree branches and the ringing of Jillian's high, clear laughter, as if the sounds were coming from somewhere much farther away. Looking through Jillian's eyes, Ronan could tell that she and Anthony were walking around the lake. Just as he'd been taught, Ronan concentrated deeply, willing the memory to become brighter. As he focused, he could feel all the places where the scene almost faded completely. The moments were too lax, as if they were pieces of thread coming loose from the fabric of Jillian's mind. But, as much as he tried, he couldn't seem to tie the moments back down, and the scene remained washed-out and stale. His will didn't seem to have any effect on the memory at all.

"You have to *want* her to remember, Ronan," Ben said from behind him.

"I do want that! That's what I'm trying to make happen," Ronan answered.

"Not enough," Ben said. "You have to be invested. You have to love this scene and need this memory to come back to life."

"I can't get much more invested. It's not safe. I'm doing it the way they taught me."

Ben snorted in derision at that. "You can't worry about distance. You have to desperately want the memory to be strong, to be cohesive. You have to want it more than you want to be safe. You have to let that wanting overwhelm you, and then push all of that emotion right into the memory. Here, watch me."

Ben stepped around Ronan and directly in front of the memory. Then he closed his eyes. A moment later, color erupted from the scene in bright hues—the rich blue of the lake, the vivid red of a park bench, the deep black of Anthony's hair. Ronan could now see the scene clearly with the details sharply in focus. The sounds of squirrels arguing and water lapping up against rocks echoed clearly through the room. Ronan could feel the fall breeze against his skin.

He could hear a younger version of Jillian's voice telling Anthony about the time she fell through the ice as a child. Before Ronan could hear how the story ended, Ben froze the scene, pushed the memory back into place, and selected another one situated close by. He expanded it until it was as large as the previous one, and he beckoned Ronan to come stand in front of it.

"Try again," he said.

Ronan took his trainer's place squarely in front of this new memory. Here, through Jillian's eyes, Ronan could see Anthony sitting across a table at a restaurant. Ronan wasn't sure if Ben had lessened his hold on the magnetic force or if this memory was simply more powerful, but he felt even more drawn to it than the last one. He recalled his trainer's words, but they felt vague and unquantifiable. Ronan wasn't sure how to transmit them into action. He liked the crisp, clear instructions he'd received at the Academy. But he'd seen Ben at work; he was incredible. No other luminator could come close to matching him. Ronan wanted to know this work as well as his trainer did, and if that meant throwing out years of Academy training, then so be it.

Instead of dividing his focus between keeping a safe distance from the memory and forcing it to comply, he concentrated on his desire to see the memory refreshed again. As he focused, he could sense all the places where the memory felt faded and dull. *I want you to be whole,* he thought. The longer he stood there, the stronger the desire became to bring this memory back to vibrancy. He wanted to strengthen it, tie it together, fix it. He let that feeling build and build, and then he pushed that deep sense of want into the memory itself. *Be whole,* he thought again.

There was no burst of color, no rush of sound. Instead, Ronan felt the magnetism of the memory triple in intensity. He tried to resist, but he felt helpless and weightless against the strength of its tide. He found himself slipping toward the dim scene in front of him, the memory growing larger and larger until it was the only thing Ronan could see. It was like a whirlpool about to suck him underwater.

Will it hurt? he wondered dimly, and then he felt annoyed at himself for having such a cliché last thought before dying.

Just then, strong hands grabbed his shoulders and threw him to the side, out of the pullspace. Ben quickly forced the memory back down to its original size and pushed the whole cluster away until it was only a tiny pinprick of light against the dome of the workroom. He placed his fingers on Jillian's temples, and in a few seconds, the memories came flowing down from the dome and back into her head. The humming dwindled back down to a faint noise. The room was just a room again.

Ronan puked all over the floor.

8

"You what?" Eli asked, turning to stare at Ronan from the driver's seat.

"Watch the road!" Ronan urged. "I almost got sucked into a memory."

"He let you in the pullspace on your first day?"

"More than that. He let me try to revive a scene."

"Are you kidding me?! That's like, third-year work," Eli said.

"Ben's not much for rule-following."

Eli blew out his breath in appreciation. "He's kind of my hero," he said. Not because Ben put Ronan in danger. Eli wasn't Cassie. He didn't love recklessness for the sake of recklessness, but he did love a good rebel. Risk for its own sake was stupidity; but risk to break rules, well, that was just fun. He couldn't help but like someone who would flout the traditions of the Council with such total disregard.

It was why he'd befriended Ronan on his first day at the Academy. Ronan's very existence at the school stood in the face of centuries of tradition and rules about lumination. Eli was drawn in like a moth to the flame. He remembered Ronan's look of surprise as he walked up to him in the cafeteria and said, "So *you're* the kid my parents have been taking antacids over for the past two weeks. Haven't had a new luminator at the Academy for a few years. I think they were hoping you all were dying out. Man, you have no idea how much easier you've made my life. With you to distract them, they've barely noticed my sub-par lumination skills lately. Not that it's my fault. Too much inbreeding. Is this seat taken?"

Even after four years, his friendship with Ronan still pissed his parents off. They were hoping that Eli's time at the Academy would make him take his gifting more seriously, help him forge connections with the *right kind* of people, and in general, stop disappointing them. Instead, he'd become friends with the very last person in his class that they would approve of, and it was the icing on the cake when he starting bringing Alister Murdoch's daughter around a few months later.

These were the small mutinies Eli allowed himself against his parents' wishes. He thought it was only fair, since they'd decided his future without consulting him. He wouldn't go so far as to tell his parents—or anyone else—that he had no desire to be a luminator. No, living without choices was the price he paid to eat his parents' food, live in his parents' house, and enjoy his parents' conditional love. He wasn't ready to change up the transaction yet. Maybe he loved rebels so much because when it came right down to it, he didn't have enough guts to be one himself—at least not where it mattered.

He drummed his fingers against the steering wheel of his Mercedes. "I *knew* I should have waited for an apprenticeship offer from a crazy recluse," Eli said. "What was it like?"

Ronan hesitated for a moment. "I threw up afterwards."

"No shame in that," Eli said. "Since you thought your life was ending and everything. Though I don't remember puking when my kayak was heading straight for those razor-sharp rocks..."

"No, you were too busy choking on water and screaming for me to save you," Ronan said.

"Those were Cassie's screams," Eli replied.

"Good. Cassie's name is coming up in normal conversation again. I wasn't sure how long that would take. You seemed pretty pissed the other night."

"I was," Eli said. "Still am, sort of, but we both know if I didn't say yes to tonight, Cassie would have called and texted me relentlessly until I gave her the chance to make it up to me."

"True," Ronan replied. "She left me seventeen messages after the cliff-jumping debacle last summer."

Eli was actually grateful that Cassie had a history of never being able to let her friends stay mad at her for long. It gave him the perfect excuse to quickly accept her invitation to what she called a "night of apologies and mayhem" when the true reason was much simpler. He missed her.

Ever since he'd met Cassie, he hated going any length of time without seeing her or at least talking to her. Her absence made everything feel off-kilter in his life, as if she was some kind of counterweight, keeping things stable. But then again, being around her also made him feel off-balance. She could throw her head back and laugh with pure, contagious joy, or give him that half-annoyed, half-amused look in the middle of one of their arguments, and Eli would feel the ground grow unsteady beneath him. So there was no winning.

They pulled up the long driveway in front of Cassie's white cottage. The house wasn't exactly small, but the mass amount of land around it made the cottage look tiny by comparison. Eli loved this home, and not just because of one of its inhabitants. There was something refreshingly understated and warm about the large front porch, tall windows, and light blue shutters. Eli always thought of it as much more welcoming than his own home, with its imposing grey stone and high walls. This cottage invited guests in; Eli's house weighed people down with its overbearing self-importance.

"You were right, about kayaking the other night," Eli said as he parked the car. "I should have agreed with you."

"But you didn't," Ronan said.

"I know. God, why is it so hard to go against Cass?"

"You guys argue all the time," Ronan said. "You think you'd have enough practice."

Eli shrugged. "That's different. That's just talk. I never seem to be able to stop her from *doing* anything once she sets her mind to it. And most of the time, that's okay. But then there are the times like earlier this week…"

After getting home from Tudic Lake the other night, once he'd calmed down, Eli had realized that he was mostly angry at himself. He knew that Cassie was always going to have these crazy ideas—some fun, some idiotic.

He thought by now, he should be able convince her of the difference. Maybe if he challenged her once in a while, she'd notice him in the same way he'd noticed her since that day at the Academy over three years ago.

"I'm not sure anyone has the power to keep Cassie from doing what she's decided to do," Ronan said as they stepped up to the front porch.

"At least you try. When it's a time like the other night, I need to start trying too." Eli said.

"Knowing Cassie, you'll probably get the chance in about two minutes," Ronan replied as he knocked.

Cassie opened the door, dressed in a full-length, slinky dark blue evening gown that was covered in sequins. She wore white gloves that came up to her elbows, and had a purple feather boa draped across her shoulders. Adele stood next to her in a looser-fitting green and gold striped dress that came down to her knees. Both girls wore bright blush and dark eyeliner.

Eli's mouth went dry when he saw Cassie. The dress clung to her, accentuating her curves, and the blue of her eyes looked even brighter than normal with the contrast of her makeup and the color of her gown.

"You guys look ridiculous," Eli said when he could speak again.

"Hey, just because this is an apology dinner doesn't mean you get to hurl insults," Cassie said lightly. "These are our costumes." She twirled around once. "It's the 1920s, we're in New York City, and there has been a *murder*. Don't worry. I have costumes for you guys too. You can get pretty much anything off Amazon."

Ronan and Eli both looked at her blankly.

"It's a murder mystery dinner," Adele supplied helpfully.

Eli groaned. "I'm beginning to wish I'd drowned."

"I'm confused," Ronan said. "Did you think doing something completely lame would cancel out doing something dangerous? Because it doesn't work like that."

"How is this an apology?" Eli asked.

Cassie rolled her eyes, grabbed them each by an arm, and pulled them inside. Eli's skin tingled where her gloved hand touched him.

"It's an apology because I'm making you dinner, and I'm doing something that doesn't put anyone's life in danger. So stop complaining."

"Under no circumstances am I wearing a costume tonight," Eli said.

After a few minutes of fruitless wheedling, Cassie shelved the topic of costumes and led them all back to the spacious dining room. Two fondue pots sat in the middle of the large oak table on top of portable burners. Platters of food surrounded the pots. Some were piled high with mini meatballs, sausage, diced chicken, and steak cubes; others contained cut-up potatoes, broccoli, carrots, and cauliflower. There were two baskets full of different types of breads and rolls, and one large serving tray near the edge of the table contained an array of strawberries, pineapple, banana, brownie chunks, biscuits, and mini cupcakes.

Eli surveyed the spread in front of him. He couldn't believe Cassie remembered the off-hand comment he'd made months ago about wanting to try fondue. He glanced up at her.

"See," she said, catching his gaze. "It *is* an apology."

"I'm not sure they did fondue in New York City in the 1920s," Ronan remarked.

"Anyways," Cassie said, pointedly ignoring Ronan's comment. "This food is only for the willing, appropriately-dressed participants of tonight's festivities."

Eli groaned again. "Okay, let's make a deal. Ronan and I will wear the stupid costumes, as long as the murder mystery doesn't start until *after* dinner."

"I think I can make that sacrifice to eat in peace," Ronan agreed.

"Ugh, fine," Cassie said, but Eli could tell she wasn't really annoyed at all.

RONAN DIDN'T like being ignored. This was a new revelation to him. At the Academy, quite a few people liked to pretend he didn't exist, and he rarely let it get to him. He used to pride himself on how little he cared about what they thought. He had important work to do; he didn't have time to waste on caring about other people's opinions of him. Before tonight, he would have said being ignored didn't really bother him. But now, he realized that it all depended on who was doing the ignoring.

Adele was right next to him at the table, and yet from the way she was acting, she might as well be sitting next to an empty seat. While she seemed happy enough to answer Cassie's questions and laugh at Eli's jokes, she never turned to include Ronan in the conversation, and she gave the briefest responses to his questions.

When he'd asked her how Cassie had gotten Adele to forgive her, she mumbled something about Cassie's persistence. But when Eli asked her the same thing, she laughed and told him how Cassie had written fifty-four apology post-it notes and had hidden them all over the guest room where Adele was staying. Ronan tried to convince himself that he was being overly-sensitive, and that it didn't make any real difference whether she acknowledged him or not, but his mind wouldn't leave it alone.

He thought they'd finally started to get along the other night, and if anything, shouldn't sharing the experience of saving the lives of two people bring them closer together? Wouldn't most girls be the least bit impressed by his act of bravery? Instead, she was treating him just like when Cassie had introduced them. Worse, actually. Because at least that time, she'd made eye contact and spoke to him. What had he done to make them start back at square...zero? Why did it matter so much to him either way?

And how—when she was wearing a ribbon around her head with a large pink feather sticking out of one side, and when her makeup looked more like she was about to walk out on stage than out in public—did that whole costume still somehow look so good on her?

"What do you think, Ronan?" Cassie's voice broke into his thoughts.

"Hm, what?" he asked.

"About going potholing. In the middle of the day. With the appropriate safety gear," Cassie said, glancing quickly over at Adele. "Is that adventurous and yet responsible enough?"

"Sure," Ronan said. "We haven't explored any of these caves in a while."

"Adele?" Cassie asked. "This way you can see another part of the island, and your life will only be put in a relative amount of danger."

Ronan glanced over at Adele and thought he saw the briefest look of fear in her eyes, but then it was gone.

"I'm game," she said airily.

Ronan heard the front door open and close again. A moment later, Cassie's father appeared at the front of the dining room, looking surprised to see people seated at his table. His presence seemed to fill up the entire room. He was at least six feet tall, broad-shouldered, barrel-chested, with shoulder-length brown hair streaked with grey. It wasn't just his size, though, that made him impressive. The man had a kind of magnetism about him; when he walked into a room, he drew everyone's gaze.

Ronan could have kissed Eli for keeping them out of costume during dinner. The last thing he wanted was for Alister Murdoch—one of the most famous men on the island, the champion of the new luminators, and Ronan's idol—to see him dressed in whatever ridiculous getup Cassie had picked out. Even though he'd interacted with Alister many times over the past three years, he could never quite seem to get over his nervous excitement whenever he was in the same room as him.

"Dad!" Cassie exclaimed, sounding instantly younger. Ronan heard the eagerness in her voice. Though she often made fun of him for his hero-worship of her father, Ronan knew he had nothing on Cassie when it came to idolizing Alister Murdoch. She lit up whenever she was near him.

"Hi sweetheart," Alister said, coming over to kiss her on the top of her head. "Wow, what a feast," he said as he looked around the table. Ronan thought he saw Alister's eyes tighten as his gaze passed over Eli. Cassie swore that her father had no problem with Eli, and he did always treat him civilly, but with how difficult the old families had made life for Alister for so many years, Ronan wondered if he couldn't help but feel resentment toward anyone in the Brennington line. Not everyone could see people as separate from their families.

Though he looked worn out from the day, Alister sat down to eat with them. Soon, he had them all laughing at stories from his time at the Academy, including the time he stumbled onto two of the professors getting *quite* friendly in the back of the library, who then tried to convince Alister that one had simply tripped and fallen on top of the other.

For every funny story though, Ronan thought Alister had to be glossing over ten painful ones. Ronan knew that Cassie's dad had been the first in his family with the luminator ability. His parents had moved into this cottage when he was young, and he'd manifested the gifting a few years later. If the Academy was still prejudiced toward outsiders when Ronan was there, he couldn't imagine how deep the animosity ran in Alister's day.

Alister went on to tell them stories about his time working for a cleaning company to make ends meet when he was first starting out as a fully-licensed luminator. From his tone, Ronan could tell that Alister was both proud and frustrated by that time. It was admirable that he'd been willing to do whatever was necessary to pursue his gifting, but Ronan thought that maybe it still bothered him, even after all this time, that others had made it so difficult for him in the first place.

When there was finally a lull in the conversation, Ronan couldn't keep himself from mentioning the upcoming election.

"Sir, did you see the latest article they wrote about you in the *Islayne Times?* They think it's looking likely that you'll win a Council seat this year."

Alister smiled at him, but Ronan thought it looked the least bit patronizing. *Of course he's seen the article*, Ronan thought, feeling foolish. *He has his own PR rep.*

"I think I did see something about that, but I try not to pin too much hope on the press. They've said similar things in years past, and it hasn't happened so far. And Ronan, *please* stop calling me sir."

"Yes, sir. I mean, I'll try. But you've never had so much support as this year," Ronan continued. "With how many new luminators have joined the ranks recently, I think you really do have a fighting chance."

"Here's hoping," Eli said flippantly. "My parents are starting to pay far too much attention to me again. It would help me out a lot if they had something else to divert their focus—losing the majority of the Council would do nicely."

"I'll be sure to put being a distraction to your parents as foremost in my motivations for running," Alister said dryly.

"I'd appreciate it," Eli said, raising his glass and giving Alister his most charming smile.

Ronan saw Cassie roll her eyes. "If we're done talking about the election, we do have a mystery to solve," she proclaimed, holding up a set of notecards in her hands.

Alister got up from the table. "As much as I'd love to stay and watch, I still have work to finish in the study." He patted Cassie's head affectionately and then left.

The room immediately felt dimmer in the wake of his departure.

"Now on to the *fun* part of the evening," Cassie said, a little too brightly, as if trying to mask her own disappointment over her father's absence.

"Hold up," Adele said. "I'm curious. What's the big deal about getting a seat on the…what is it called again, the Council?"

"How can you not know that?" Ronan asked incredulously. "Haven't you been coming here for years?"

Adele shrugged, looking over at Cassie.

"*Excuse me* if I didn't want to bore her with useless facts about the Council. I found better things for us to do with our time." Cassie flicked one of the cards, looking annoyed.

Ronan rolled his eyes at her. "Alister getting a seat on the Lumin Council is a huge deal because—"

"How about I explain it?" Eli cut him off. "Because if you get up on this soapbox, it'll take forever, and then we'll never get around to Cassie's lame murder mystery. Which wait, on second thought, go ahead Ronan."

Cassie jabbed her fondue fork at Eli menacingly.

"Ah, don't stab me woman. I was only joking," Eli said. "For as far back as anyone can remember, the old families—that would be my own dear bloodline, and our kin, the Lydons and the Roscoes—have been in service to the rulers of Islayne, in exchange for wealth and protection. Since only people on our land manifested the power, we were able to keep the trade closed to anyone outside of the families. Though my relatives at times fought and bickered with one another, they got used to being the ones who called the shots of the trade.

"Then, in the late 1800's, when the current owners of the island decided they couldn't afford luminator services anymore, my kin became quite entrepreneurial—it's amazing what we're capable of when someone threatens our polished silver and elaborate cocktail parties. The Lydons took out massive loans to found the Academy, begin the Council, and build a few luminator offices. But turns out having money doesn't necessitate being good with it, and they underestimated how long it would take for them to start making a profit from lumination. When the Lydons defaulted on the loan, the bank took quite a big chunk of our property and sold it to developers. They, in turn, cut up that land into smaller estates, like this one," Eli said, indicating Cassie's home. "And eventually some of those estates were turned into neighborhoods, like the one Ronan lives in."

"At first, when some of the new residents began to develop the gifting, my relatives just saw it as a nuisance, not a threat. I guess they thought all of the residents of Islayne would be as easy to control as any of the servants or tenants on the family land who'd developed the gifting in the past. My beloved ancestors had managed to keep any of them from practicing through threat of eviction or loss of livelihood, so maybe they'd thought it wouldn't be that difficult to keep the trade closed to everyone else on the island. Turned out they were wrong, again. I would have loved to see my great-grandparents' faces on the day the first new luminator was allowed to attend the Academy."

"You? Take pleasure in someone else's pain? Never," Cassie said.

"I thought that was the definition of family," Eli said, shooting her a quick grin. "Now stop interrupting, or we'll never get to your dumb game. Okay, where was I? My relatives started to lose their stranglehold on the trade. When they opened lumination to the public, one of the ways they legitimized it was establishing the Council. As the ruling body over luminators, the Council distributed clients according to seniority and yearly ranking, exacted licensing fees, and regulated the teachings of the Academy, which they started up around the same time. The Council also created and enforced stricter codes of conduct, most importantly, the law that no one could practice the trade without a license."

"Once these new luminators started coming out of the woodworks, the Council supposedly amended its laws to allow for them to also start receiving their fair share of clients and compensation.

"But us old families, we're pretty crafty. And pretty corrupt. Except for yours truly, of course. We lost the battle over the Academy, but since then, we've found tons of workarounds and loopholes—incredibly high workspace rent, keeping new luminators from taking on apprentices, excessive licensing fees, convoluted standards of practice—anything and everything you could think of to keep the deck quite well-stacked in our favor. And part of the reason we've been so successful so far is how easily most members on the Council bow to our inbred wills."

"Why doesn't the Council stand up to the families?" Adele asked.

"Money and connections, my friend. It's all the rage here. It also helps that a good many Council appointees still have some old family blood in their veins. And you have to remember, we don't have *all* of the members in our pocket. We have just enough, at this point, to tip the rulings in our favor. Which is why everyone I'm related to is so against Alister's campaign. If he manages to win a seat, the majority of the Council will no longer be bought off by the old families, and new legislation can be passed to make it much fairer for the new luminators."

"So, what will that mean?" Adele asked. "Like, they won't have to pay as high of a fee to practice?"

Now Ronan couldn't help himself from jumping in. "If Alister gets his way, then it could mean a world of change for the new luminators—most of them could afford to practice full time, it would be much easier for them to take on apprentices, they wouldn't have to choose between the work they love and putting enough food on the table. At the very least, it would even the playing field between the old families and the new luminators. They would have a fighting chance to be judged on the basis of their abilities and not their heritage. But it all rides on Alister's ability to win a Council seat. He's the only one who has even close to enough support."

"Thus, Ronan's obsessive love for the man," Eli said.

"*Obsessive love* is putting it a bit strongly," Ronan said. "I just think that—"

"No, no, no more," Cassie said, cutting Ronan off. "I'm stopping all talk of my dad, or the election, or the Council. Otherwise you guys will go on forever."

"Why do you always get so annoyed when we start talking about this?" Ronan asked Cassie, not bothering to hide his irritation. "It's important.

This could affect my whole future—not to mention Eli's and your dad's. Would it kill you to take an interest in the trade?"

A quick look of resentment passed over Cassie's face, but then it was gone. She spread her hands out in front of her. "I'm sorry that my life doesn't begin and end at the Lumin District, Ronan. What do you want me to say? I don't have the gifting. It gets old when we talk about it all the time."

"You're best friends with *two* apprentices, and your dad is one of the most famous luminators on the island. How can you not care?"

"Enough with the accusations. I do care," she said. "It's just—other things matter more to me. I'm sorry for cutting you off, okay?" she said. "I know this stuff means a lot to you. But you have to admit that conversation could have gone on forever, and we have a game to get to."

"Fine," Ronan replied. He knew he wasn't being totally fair. Cassie did show an interest in the trade, much more so than a lot of other people who didn't have the gifting. But sometimes, it didn't feel genuine to him. Either way, he should be used to it by now; he didn't know why her interruption frustrated him so much tonight. Maybe it was just the combination of one friend's current apathy toward his future and another's apparent apathy toward his entire existence that was making him irritable.

"Sorry, Cass, I started it," Adele said glancing between her and Ronan. *So she does know I'm here.* Ronan thought. "But I'm good with the history lesson now. We can proceed with our evening."

"Finally," Cassie said, standing up from the table and holding her hands up theatrically. "We're in New York City, it's 1922, and there's been a *murder...*"

9

Ronan and Eli stood on the Murdoch's small private dock, about a quarter of a mile away from Cassie's house. Ronan fidgeted impatiently. He looked out at the choppy, brilliant blue surf of the ocean, and then he checked the time on his phone again. After five straight days of his apprenticeship with Ben, it felt strange to stand still. It also felt strange to have a conversation that didn't include a constant string of sarcastic remarks or random questions on luminator history, the latest trade stats, or some minutia of complex Council proceedings.

The week had been long and exhausting and exhilarating. Ben put Ronan through a myriad of mind-strengthening exercises each day, that is when he wasn't too busy interrogating Ronan on luminator terminology or insulting his conventional intelligence. But Ronan found that the more time he spent with Ben, the less his mockery bothered him. In fact, he was starting to appreciate it. Since Ben had thrown out all the rules of common courtesy, now there was more room to relax and concentrate on what was important.

Ronan was frustrated that Ben hadn't let him try to brighten another memory yet. When he asked his trainer about it during Jillian's last session, Ben snorted and said until Ronan could learn to control the contents of his stomach, he didn't have any business reviving memories. But Ben did continue to allow him in the pullspace, so for now, Ronan contented himself to watch and learn from his trainer's mastery of the trade.

His long days in Ben's office made their murder mystery game at Cassie's house feel like months ago, even though it was only the previous weekend. Of course, maybe Ronan was blocking it from his mind since the game ended up being as lame as Ronan and Eli had said it would be. Cassie claimed it was their fault, since she said the mystery could only be as interesting and entertaining as the participants. Eli had cheerfully pointed out that such a trait was the mark of a boring game.

At least now they were going to do something exciting. After last weekend, Ronan was in favor of Cassie always planning life-threatening adventures over any more game nights. Of course, it'd still be nice if the escapade could start on time. He glanced down at his phone again.

"Why do we ever get to places when Cassie tells us to?" Ronan asked. "You think we'd learn by now that she's always late."

"Hope springs eternal, I guess," Eli answered.

Finally, Cassie's blue Expedition drove up the small dirt path, two more kayaks tied to the top—with Cassie's love for exploring Islayne, the Murdochs seemed to have an unending supply of water sport equipment at their house. Cassie parked the car, jumped out, and pulled an overloaded backpack from the trunk. Even at this distance, Ronan could see that she was bouncing with enthusiasm, though Adele didn't seem to share her excitement. Ronan and Eli walked back toward the car to help with the kayaks.

Eli and Cassie soon fell into their usual routine of bickering, this time over the best way to secure kayaks to the top of a car. Ronan noticed that Adele looked pale, and she kept stealing glances at Cassie's backpack of caving gear like something was about to jump out of it and attack her at any moment.

"Hey, are you okay?" Ronan asked her, reaching out and barely touching her shoulder. She started and pulled back from him.

"What? Oh, yeah, I'm fine. God, you scared me."

"Sorry. You just look like...well, not good."

"What every girl loves to hear," she said.

"No, I mean, you always look *good*."

"Hm?" she asked, her eyebrows raised.

"I'm trying to say you look worried."

"Well, I'm fine," she said, sounding as if she was trying to convince herself. "I am fine."

"Hey, are you guys going to help or just stand there?" Cassie called over to them.

As Ronan helped to pull one kayak off the top of Cassie's SUV, he tried to determine what was worse—being ignored or having an incredibly awkward interaction where he told a girl that she looked terrible and then corrected himself by saying she *always* looked good. He still hadn't decided by the time they got the kayaks in the water and began paddling parallel to the shore, Eli and Cassie in front, Adele and Ronan following behind.

After a few stilted efforts at starting a conversation with Adele, Ronan gave up, and they paddled in silence. Maybe he'd just imagined that they'd started getting along a few weeks ago at Tudic Lake. Adele had probably just been making a huge effort to be nice to Cassie's friends, and now she'd given up on Ronan. But why? Had he done something to turn her off or annoy her? He didn't think it was possible since they hadn't had a real conversation since kayaking together. But what did he know?

He wrestled with these thoughts as they glided along the water, trailing behind Cassie and Eli. As they rounded the northern edge of the island—the section of land still owned by the old families—the rocky beaches along the coast gave way to sheer cliff face. In a few more minutes, they came upon a wide break in the rock. As they changed directions and paddled toward the opening, the water gradually became shallow again, and soon all four of them got out and pulled the kayaks up onto the narrow swatch of sand at the mouth of a cave.

Cassie jumped out. "Cool, huh? I found this opening a few weeks back. It leads back to a whole network of caves. Maybe some of them have never even been explored."

"You came out here by yourself?" Eli asked.

"Mayyybe," Cassie answered. "But this time I'm here with you guys, in the middle of the day, and with the safety equipment. So, growth."

Eli just shook his head, then he grabbed a headlamp and a roll of brightly colored tape from his backpack. "I'll be back in a minute," he said, walking into the cave.

"Addy, what's wrong?" Cassie asked. Adele was staring into the mouth of the cave, and her face was even paler than before. She seemed to be struggling to breathe normally.

"I'm, I'm fine. Just, give me a minute," she said.

"What's going on?" Cassie asked, coming to her side.

Adele leaned over now, her hands on her knees. She didn't say anything for a few minutes, just kept trying to take a deep breath. Finally, she stood back up.

"I'm insanely claustrophobic," she said.

"What? Are you serious?" Cassie asked. "I never knew that. Why didn't you say anything before?"

"I don't like to talk about it much, and I didn't want to ruin this for you. I could tell you were so excited. Maybe I should just wait here until you guys are done."

"No, that's dumb," Cassie said. "We are not leaving you here. We'll just head back."

"No, *that's* dumb. We came all the way out here. We are not turning back just for me," Adele said, leaning back against the rock wall at the entrance to the cave.

It was strange to see her this way—vulnerable, anxious, scared. Ronan was used to her angry side, and her collected, easygoing side, and, most recently, her completely-ignoring-him side, but not this. In a weird way, it made him like her more.

"I can stay out here with you," Ronan offered. "Seen one cave, you've seen them all."

Adele looked him in the eyes for the first time all day. She seemed grateful.

"Thank you," she said, taking a deep breath. "But, it's okay, I'm doing okay now. I think I should try to do it. I want to. Not just for you, Cass, but for me. That's the other reason I didn't tell you—I was hoping if I just didn't say anything and forced myself to do it, then it wouldn't be as bad. I don't want this to keep me from doing stuff."

"Are you sure?" Cassie asked. "We can seriously just head back."

"Yeah, I'm sure. And if I run out screaming in a few minutes, we'll know it was too much, too soon." Adele said, a little of the color returning to her face.

"Pee break completed," Eli said as he walked back toward them, holding up the tape. "And I marked the spot very clearly with this stuff, so if you step in it, you really only have yourself to blame. Why do you all look like someone died?"

"One day, you're going to say that, and someone *will* have just died," Cassie said.

"Then I'll be able to congratulate myself on such a fine-tuned ability to read faces."

She rolled her eyes. "Well your ability is not very fine-tuned right now. Nothing's the matter."

Cassie dug the other headlamps out of the backpack and tossed one to Ronan and one to Adele. Ronan saw Adele shoot Cassie a grateful look as she caught it. As they headed toward the cave entrance, Cassie pulled Ronan aside and let Adele and Eli walk ahead.

"Keep an eye on her, okay?" she asked. "I'm the only one who's been here before, so I'm going to take the lead. Will you make sure Adele doesn't totally lose it in there?"

"If you want," Ronan shrugged. "I don't know how much of a help I'll be. I don't think she likes me that much."

Cassie snorted once in reply and then ran to catch up to the others.

As Ronan followed her inside, from the light of his headlamp he could see five different cave openings. Without hesitating, Cassie chose the widest one farthest to the left. As they walked further inside, Eli marked their progress every few hundred feet with the tape. Cassie made him promise to take it all off on the way back, so they didn't detract from what she called "the integrity of the cave."

Ronan purposefully matched Adele's slower pace as Cassie and Eli got further ahead of them. After a few minutes of uncomfortable silence, Ronan asked, "Are you doing okay? With the whole caving thing?"

She nodded slightly. "Yeah, okay."

Ronan searched for a comforting thought to share. "Look how big this tunnel is. Hard to imagine these walls closing in." He immediately wished the words back as he felt Adele tense up next to him. "Sorry! That was definitely not the right thing to say in this situation."

"No, it's okay. I know it's stupid to be scared of this."

"Hey, everyone has weird fears, right?"

"What's yours?"

He hesitated for a brief moment. "I am terrified of choking to death."

"Are you serious?" she asked.

"Dead serious. I think about it every time I eat a carrot too quickly."

"Well, don't eat them then."

"But I love carrots."

"Then eat them slower."

"Somehow I always end up being in a hurry while snacking."

"Okay now if you choke to death, I'm going to have to say you tempted fate one too many times."

"Fair enough," he said.

Adele craned her head up. "It does help, this tunnel being so big." She seemed to relax a bit.

"I'll speak to the tour guide company—see if that can't be arranged every time we go exploring unknown territory," Ronan said.

There was her short, accidental laugh again. Warmth spread through Ronan's chest at the sound.

"While you're at it," she replied. "See if they can throw in a discovery or two of rare jewels. Or gold. I'm not picky."

"Maybe not picky, but definitely cliché. Come on, everybody finds gold or jewels. If you're going to request a discovery, at least choose something unique."

"Nope. Some things are cliché for a reason. You can have your rare finding. I'll be more than happy with my run-of-the-mill buried treasure."

"Have it your way," he said. "I was just trying to keep life interesting for you."

"With all the gold, I can buy interesting."

"But could you—"

Ronan's words broke off as they turned a sharp corner. The corridor they'd been walking in for the past half hour opened abruptly into a massive cavern. Whatever Ronan was about to say fled from his mind as quickly the view changed from a rock wall to the expansive, breathtaking scenery of the expansive chamber in front of him.

Large beams of light streamed through from different openings near the top of the cavern, at least two hundred feet above their heads. Portions of the cave ceiling looked like they had partially melted into thousands of rock icicles. They were called *stalactites*, Ronan recalled dimly from his geology class last year. The streams of light revealed a large pool on one side of the cavern. The water looked bright greenish-blue, refracting the brilliant colors of the rocks along the pool's bottom.

For a few minutes, the four of them said nothing. They stood unmoving and took in the majesty of the view in front of them. Ronan thought briefly that if this didn't change Adele's opinion of Islayne, then nothing would. But even as he recognized the beauty of the cavern, Ronan couldn't help but feel that something was off about the place. Slowly, they made their way further in, stepping gingerly as if they could somehow damage the splendor of the place by hurry or heavy footfalls. There was enough light in the cavern to see without the use of headlamps, so they all took them off. Ronan brushed his hand against one side of the cavern wall, tracing the rough stone with his fingertips, wondering if anyone else had ever touched it before him.

But that same feeling kept nagging at him, the reason for it staying just outside of his reach. He looked around again, trying to figure out the source of his misgiving. Then it dawned on him—there was a faint but distinct hum in the air, a sound only produced by a memory session.

10

"If someone's been practicing here in secret, that has to violate at least a dozen Council laws…"

Adele tried to focus on what Ronan was saying. It seemed like a big deal. But she kept getting distracted by his furrowed brow and the intensity in his eyes. He got so serious when he talked about lumination. Adele always thought she didn't like serious guys—she never understood the appeal of the strong, silent type—but now she realized it was that she didn't like guys who took *themselves* too seriously. Someone who believed in something as deeply as Ronan did lumination, well, that was kind of hot.

She let her gaze slide over his shoulders, across the compact muscles in his arms, and down to his hands. They were elongated, almost delicate, like the hands of a piano player. She wondered what it would feel like for those hands to stroke her face, to see that look in his eyes up close…

Stop it, she told herself. *That is not going to happen.* When she'd first laid eyes on Ronan at the bookstore, she thought he was cute. He had the whole intense eyes, tousled dark hair thing going for him, but that was quickly pushed from her mind by how bizarre and rude he'd acted toward her. He didn't win many points the next time they talked either, telling her that her memories wouldn't be worth the effort. But after that comment, they'd started to get along that night. The conversation flowed easily between them. Adele couldn't remember the last time she'd found it so easy to talk to someone she barely knew. She remembered the determination in his eyes as she steadied him on the rock by the cliff edge, and she saw the relief clearly on his face once they pulled Eli and Cassie safely from the rough water. She'd had the ridiculous thought that she hoped he'd look like that if she were ever pulled back from the brink of danger.

It wasn't just his knack for saving his friends' lives, either. Ronan knew exactly what he wanted to do with his life, something she didn't think was very common in guys her age. He had a refreshing surety about him. At times, it tipped into annoying arrogance, but for the most part, she found it intriguing. He had been genuinely apologetic about the way he treated her at the bookstore, and he was so kind, like earlier today, offering to stay out with her on the beach...

And this—the fact that she couldn't seem to be able to keep her mind from going over and over his good qualities—was exactly why she'd had to turn him down. She didn't need another conversation with him keeping her awake tonight. She forced herself to concentrate on Ronan's words.

"So, should we tell the Council?" Ronan asked, glancing around at everyone.

"Would they care?" Adele asked as she avoided looking directly at Ronan. "Last weekend, you guys made such a big deal about them being corrupt."

"Selectively corrupt. Only when it comes to new luminators," Eli answered. "The Council—and my extended family, for that matter—take the reputation of lumination very seriously. And part of that reputation is the protection of our clients. But I don't know what they would do about this. That noise is so faint—whoever practiced here, it must have been a long time ago. I think if we report it, we'll have piles of paperwork to fill in, and then nothing to show for it. I mean, what are they going to do, stake out the premises to see if the luminator comes back again after his ten-year hiatus?"

Cassie got up and started walking around the cavern, a slightly bewildered expression on her face.

"Cassie, where are you going?" Ronan asked, the annoyance clear in his voice. "We need to figure out what to do about this."

"I have a headache, and talking about this is making it worse." She called back over her shoulder. "I'm with Eli. Why waste our time if they aren't going to take any action?"

"Uh, yeah, unless we have something more to go on, I think we're better off leaving it alone," Eli said, and Adele caught the faint note of surprise in his voice. She thought Eli must not be very used to Cassie agreeing with him.

Ronan turned to look at Adele, raising his eyebrows. Her stomach flipped over.

"Well, if you guys say the Council won't do anything," she said. "And if it happened a long time ago, then I guess, what's the point?" She was surprised at how matter-of-fact her voice sounded when she felt anything but matter-of-fact with Ronan's eyes on her.

He turned away, looking like he was still internally debating the issue. But eventually he nodded. "Yeah, I guess there's nothing we can do."

Eli jumped up. "Are we dismissed sir?" he asked, saluting Ronan.

"Hey guys! Come over here!" Cassie called from the other side of the cavern.

The breathless excitement in Cassie's voice took Adele back to so many other times when she'd heard that same tone. She was nine years old, and Cassie held a needle and half an apple in her hands, soon after they'd watched the scene in *The Parent Trap* where one twin pierces the other's ear. Three years ago, Cassie woke her up early in the morning so they could explore the ruins of the monastery on the southern side of Islayne as the sun rose. Last fall, as Cassie told her about the famous treasure hunt for *La Chouette D'or*, and they decided they would take a graduation trip to France in two years to join in the search for the golden owl. And then just a few weeks ago, when Adele called to tell her about staying on Islayne for the whole summer.

That tone almost made Adele okay with the fact that her mum had shipped her off to the island without a second thought as to how her only daughter might feel about the arrangement under the circumstances.

She followed Ronan and Eli over to a grinning Cassie, who was standing next to a large hole near the edge of the cavern.

"I don't know how deep this goes. I think we should find out," Cassie said, running back over to the front of the cavern where she'd left her backpack. Her headache had apparently not dimmed her sense of adventure.

Adele stepped up close to the edge of the shaft. She guessed it spanned about six feet across. Holding her headlamp in her hands, she shined the light into the dark expanse beneath her. She could see a few ledges jutting out from the rough rock that comprised the sides, but the hole stretched much further down than her light could reach. She took a step back, shuddering at the thought of falling into such a small space, being trapped in the utter darkness where she couldn't even stretch out both hands without touching rock walls. Close enough to suffocate. She leaned forward, putting her hands on her knees. Her breath starting coming in short gasps.

"Adele, breathe. It's okay," said a voice next to her. She felt Ronan's hand on her back. Even in her state of half-panic, his touch sent a shiver down her spine. He led her over to the wall of the cavern—a good twenty feet away from the hole—and made her sit down.

She closed her eyes and took a few deep breaths, trying to calm down. She reminded herself that she was in a massive cavern, with light spilling in above. She was not in a small dark hole. She had plenty of air and plenty of room. She was okay. She was okay.

"Do you need water, or something?" Ronan asked, sitting down next to her. She looked up to see the worry in his grey eyes, and her breath caught for a wholly different reason.

"No, I'm okay now, thanks. Sorry, I uh, made the mistake of imagining life at the bottom of a small hole. Not the best idea for a claustrophobic caver." She smiled weakly.

Cassie jogged back over with an armful of rope, a harness, and a few complicated-looking metal climbing devices. Then she caught sight of Adele's face, hurried over to her, and dropped the equipment. "Oh Adele, I'm sorry. I didn't think about that scaring you. Do we need to go?"

"No, no, it's okay," Adele said, finally feeling able to breathe normally again. "Minor freak out over. But, do you know what you're doing with all of that, Cassie?" Adele gestured to the equipment littering the cavern floor.

"The shaft runs deep, and it's not very wide." She said with a slight, involuntary shudder.

"Remember that rappelling class I took at the rec center a few years back?" Cassie asked. "Well, single rope technique was a big part of it." She picked up two of the metal pieces off the floor and held one up to Adele. "This is my Petzl Stop, it's a kind of descender, for climbing down the rope, and this"—she indicated the other metal piece—"is the ascender, a Petzl Croll, for climbing back up. I even got my class 1 certification." Cassie flashed her a grin.

Adele imagined descending into that small, dark space with only some rope and metal tethering her to the surface. She shuddered again. "Okay, just, be careful, please," she called after Cassie as her friend walked over to the edge of the hole. She and Eli soon had the rope securely tied to a thick slab of rock. Then Cassie tightened her harness, clipped the various metal contraptions in place, and slowly leaned back over the edge.

Adele looked away. "I can't watch this," she said.

"She really does know what she's doing," Ronan reassured her. "Trust me, all I heard about for weeks after that stupid class was the pros and cons of the Jumar versus the Petzl Croll, the best kind of rope, the importance of rigging points, blah, blah blah. I learned more than I ever wanted to about rappelling."

She laughed. "Yeah, Cassie never was one for keeping things to herself."

"I know. I never quite understood that," Ronan said, idly playing with some pebbles on the cavern floor. Adele found herself distracted by his hands again. She looked over to see Eli standing by the edge of the hole, fully focused on making sure Cassie was safe.

"Sharing your excitement?" she asked Ronan. "I think it's a pretty common thing."

"It's still weird to me. For Cass, it's like the more she likes something, the more the words pour out of her. But if there's something that I truly care about, it means too much to waste it in casual conversation. It has to be the right time and the right place and the right person; otherwise, it cheapens it."

Adele head snapped up to look at Ronan, taken aback by how clearly he articulated how she'd always felt about sharing things with people.

"Yes, that's...I mean, I've never heard anyone else say that before. That's exactly how I feel about it."

His eyes met hers, and she couldn't seem to look away. Suddenly, it was as if there was an electrical current in the small space between them. She could feel something unfurling in her chest as she stared into his grey eyes. And then he was leaning closer to her.

There was a small voice in the back of her head that told her to turn her head, change the subject, make a joke, get up and walk away. She couldn't do this. It wasn't fair to anyone. But she felt helpless to heed her more rational self.

"I found something!" Cassie's voice shattered the moment, bringing Adele back down to reality. They both jolted back from each other. Adele stood up without a word and walked back closer to the edge of the hole. She heard Ronan follow her, but she didn't turn to look at him. A few moments later, Cassie reached the top of the hole, and Eli helped pull her back out of it. She held a small book in her mouth.

"That is so nasty," Eli said as he saw it. "I can't believe you put that in your mouth—who knows how long it's been down there?"

"Why do you care? Planning on kissing me?" She asked lightly once she was standing and able to take the book out of her mouth. Adele thought she saw a brief shadow pass over Eli's face.

"Maybe I don't want you catching a nasty disease and then passing it along to the rest of us," Eli retorted.

"That was the best way to make sure I didn't drop it. I found it on one of the rock ledges."

Cassie gazed at the book, a puzzled expression on her face. It was leather-bound with strange markings on the front. She leafed through a couple of the pages.

"What language is this?" she asked.

"Lemme see," Eli said, his voice brightening with interest.

Eli took the book gingerly from Cassie and began to study the pages in earnest. After a few seconds, he shut the book and looked up.

"It's definitely some version of Gaelic—early, but I can't tell quite how early."

"How do you know that?" Adele asked.

Eli shrugged. "I like old languages. They're kind of my hobby. I'll need to take it home and compare it to a few of the dictionaries we have."

Eli took off his jacket, wrapped it around the book, and then stowed it in Cassie's backpack.

"Who says you get to take it home?" Cassie asked. "Pretty sure I'm the one who risked life and limb to find it."

"Relax, I'll give it back to you once I figure out what it says."

"Fine. Just don't take forever." Then she looked down at her watch. "I think we should be getting back. It's going to take us at least another half hour to walk to the kayaks, and if we wait much longer, it will be dark by the time we get out on the water."

"Wow, look at you," Ronan said. "Our little safety officer."

She shoved him lightly. "I'm still on probation from our last adventure, remember? I'm trying to make up for it."

They started to walk back toward the mouth of the cavern. Adele paused near the entrance, taking in the view one more time as Cassie and Eli passed her by.

"See," Ronan said as he came up next to Adele. "Not such a godforsaken place after all."

"What?" she asked, very aware of how close he was standing to her.

"First time I met you, that's what you said about Islayne. You called it a 'godforsaken island.'"

They followed Cassie and Eli into the corridor.

"I said that?" she asked. "I don't remember."

"Well I do. I was so surprised that anyone could think that about Islayne, I accidentally dropped a few travel guides..."

"Funny how that story keeps changing."

Adele tried to pretend that she felt completely normal and at ease as they made their way back through the tunnel. She tried to pretend that when his hand accidentally brushed lightly against the back of hers, it didn't make her skin tingle. She tried, and she failed.

"What you did today," Ronan said quietly. "Coming with us. I think it was brave."

The corners of her mouth quirked into a smile. She forced herself to take a deep breath. *Nothing has changed*, she reminded herself. *This is still a bad idea. It's not going to work.*

"We should probably hurry up," she said, hearing the strain in her tone. "I don't want Cassie to worry that we've gotten lost."

She picked up her pace, and within a few minutes, they caught up to Eli and Cassie. Adele made sure to keep some distance between her and Ronan for the rest of the evening, and she could almost convince herself that it was the best choice for everyone.

11

"Please don't throw up on my floor this time," Ben said as he stepped away from the memory and motioned for Ronan to take his place.

Ronan felt like he'd lived in this office for the past three weeks. He'd barely seen Eli, and hadn't seen Cassie or Adele at all since the four of them had gone caving. He had the nagging feeling that the girls were avoiding him, but he still didn't know what he'd done wrong. Cassie hadn't planned anything for the four of them to do together, which was unusual for her. He tried to convince himself he was being paranoid and that Cassie was just spending some one-on-one time with Adele. But from how excited she'd been for the four of them to hit it off at the beginning of the summer, the recent radio silence didn't make sense.

At least Ronan knew why he hadn't seen much of Eli lately. Between his friend's apprenticeship and his obsession over trying to translate the book he'd found in the cavern, Eli had little time to spare these past few weeks.

So instead of spending his free time exploring Islayne, Ronan found himself pouring more and more hours into his apprenticeship. He started showing up early at Ben's office every morning and didn't leave until well past closing time. Ben taught him luminator techniques that Ronan had never heard of, making him wonder if Ben had invented them himself.

Ronan would leave Ben's office each day mentally and physically exhausted, but by the time he woke up the next morning, his mind would be craving more. Though Ben was as insulting and cavalier as ever, Ronan began to learn between his jabs and sarcasm. And Ronan thought that maybe, just maybe, he was starting to earn his trainer's begrudging respect.

And now, all of that hard work might just pay off, Ronan thought as he stepped in front of the memory. He felt the magnetic pull immediately, beckoning him in. This one showed Anthony at Jillian's side at a fair in the midst of a crowd of people. Ronan took a small step closer to the frozen scene, feeling the force of the memory triple in intensity. He ignored the rising panic in his chest, just like Ben had taught him. Instead, he took a deep breath and focused all of his mental energy on capping the force and pushing back against the pull. After a few minutes, he felt the magnetic draw lessening, as if he'd just won a backwards game of tug-of-war. He breathed a little easier.

Ronan focused and allowed the scene to play, taking in the muted colors and the subdued sounds. Everything felt stale and stilted. He let his mind dwell on the dimness all around him. Ronan could sense the memory like a worn blanket fraying at the edges and the seams, about to come undone. The longer he stood there, the more he wanted to mend what was unraveling. He wanted to see the color of the gaudy carnival huts and hear the mother shouting for her child to slow down. These moments were meant to be alive and remembered, not to dwindle into oblivion.

He fed that longing, letting it balloon in his chest, and then finally, he pushed that feeling into the memory. For a moment, nothing happened. Time seemed to stand still. Ronan started to sweat from the strain of concentration and longing. Then, slowly, so much more slowly than when Ben worked, the colors began to brighten and the sounds grew slightly louder. He caught a small whiff of popcorn and saw a flash of sunlight reflected off the metal of the Ferris wheel. Ronan didn't let himself get distracted. He continued to feed the longing inside of him. *Grow brighter,* he thought. *Be whole again. Be remembered.*

Suddenly, colors burst forth from the scene. The noises of children laughing and a man yelling and obnoxious carnival music filled the workroom. Ronan could smell the sickly-sweet scent of candy floss and feel the hot summer sun beat down against the crowds. Everything was fresh and clear and thriving.

Ronan stepped back, in awe of what he'd accomplished. It didn't fill him with arrogance, but instead with a kind of humble wonder that he was able to do this. That somehow, this incredible, strange gifting had found its way into his head and his hands and his soul and allowed him to produce the beauty in front of him.

Before he had any more time to contemplate the scene, the magnetic force of the memory descended down on him like gravity. In his wonder, he'd forgotten the ever-present danger of what he was doing. *Not again*, he thought. He tried to focus his mental energy against the force, but he was drained from the effort of reviving the scene, and his mind wouldn't obey him.

Ronan began to truly panic as he felt himself weakening in the face of the memory's power. Then once again, Ben shoved him out of the pullspace and took his place. After a few seconds, the memory receded away from them. His trainer quickly funneled the mindscape back into Jillian's head, and then he ended the session.

"Here, this will help with the dizziness," Ronan said as he handed Jillian a steaming cup of tea. He tried to be as careful as possible since his hands were still shaking slightly.

She took a few small sips. "Mmm, that is delicious," she murmured. "And I love how quickly it makes the room stop spinning. What kind of tea is this?"

"It's called Longwood tea. Made from a plant that's native to the island," Ronan said absently as he eyed the front door of the office. As soon as Ben had ended the session, he'd raced out of the workroom saying that he was dying for a salmon and cream cheese bagel, one of his more normal mid-afternoon cravings. Even though Ronan was used to his trainer rushing off last minute for any number of odd reasons, he couldn't help but feel disappointed that Ben hadn't even mentioned his accomplishment. Instead, he'd left Ronan to handle Jillian's post-session time by himself.

"Are you all right, Ronan?" Jillian asked. "I can't help but notice that your hands are shaking, and you seem a bit distracted."

"It's nothing. I'm fine."

Ronan wasn't about to tell her that he was still recovering from brightening one of her memories. He had no idea how well-versed she was in Council law, but it wouldn't take much for her to discover that it wasn't exactly legal for an apprentice to rummage around in a client's mind after so little training.

"This is such a strange experience," Jillian said, looking into the unlit fireplace. "I had a friend come here a few years ago, and she tried to prepare me for what it would be like, but it's rather impossible to explain, isn't it? So much of my past has been flooding my mind lately. It's truly like traveling back in time. Lucas would have loved this."

She got his attention with that.

"Your husband?" he asked, sounding shorter than he meant to.

"Yes, my husband," she answered, meeting his gaze openly. "He always was one for new experiences and new adventures. How I loved that about him."

"Then why—" Ronan began, before stopping himself.

"Why aren't I here to remember more of him?" she finished for him.

But before she could continue, Ben walked back through the front door, wafting the strong smell of fish in along with him. He soon ushered Jillian out of the office and then told Ronan that he'd like to talk to him.

"So, do you not have any friends?" Ben asked. He sat across from Ronan on one of the recliners in the parlor. Ronan thought maybe his trainer would deign to give him a bit of encouragement, or at least bring up the fact that he'd just accomplished something no one else his age had ever done, but instead, he wanted to discuss Ronan's recent lack of a social life.

Ronan sighed. "Yes, I have friends. Why are you asking me?"

"You've been spending every waking moment at this office. And in one sense, I appreciate your dedication. But honestly, I am starting to wonder whether I'm training an anti-social loser."

After over a month of apprenticing with him, Ronan was used to Ben talking to him that way, and it normally didn't bother him. And yet this time, his words touched a nerve.

"This coming from a fifteen-year recluse?" Ronan asked.

"Exactly why I may know what I'm talking about," Ben said softly. He seemed to forget that Ronan was there for a moment, and he looked to be contemplating something far away or far in the past. For the first time, he didn't seem like the self-assured, sarcastic man that Ronan had come to expect. It was as if a mask had slipped off by accident, and underneath all Ronan could see was pain.

"What happened with your family? With the Roscoes?" Ronan asked before he could think better of it.

The question seemed to rouse Ben from his reverie. The sadness left him, and he gave Ronan a hard look.

"If you want to remain my apprentice, you will never ask me that again," he said, letting the threat hang in the air for a moment. "Now, I brought up your amount of time in the office for a reason. If you try to keep up this kind of pace, you'll burn out. It could be dangerous. You need to start spending less time here, or I will start kicking you out of sessions."

"But I can handle it!" Ronan protested. He was just starting to get a taste for the real work of lumination, and he wanted more of it, not less.

"No, you *think* you can handle it, which is not the same thing at all. We aren't discussing this. I'm telling you this. Figure out a way to have some kind of life outside of this work, or I'll start banning you from the office. I barely have time to think anymore. You're always here."

"Fine," Ronan said. This was just perfect. As a reward for working hard and brightening his first memory, Ben insulted him and made him spend less time moving toward what he wanted.

"Good. I want you to start now," Ben said.

"But I thought we were going to discuss the session and then practice the concentration exercises we started yesterday?"

"We will. Tomorrow. At noon. Which is the next time I want to see you," Ben said. "Go see some of those friends you swear you have."

12

Eli peered down at the dictionary, and then back at the leather-bound book, and then back at the dictionary. After jotting down a few more notes, he pushed the books away from him and stood up from the desk to stretch. He looked out of the massive window taking up one wall of the library. It was already dark outside. He'd been at this for hours today. Large, mahogany bookshelves lined every wall in the room and stretched two stories high. If Eli could have his way, he would spend most of his life in this library. He would get a job as some kind of historical expert, so he could pore over old books to find the answers to long-forgotten questions. He would never step foot inside a luminator office again. But that wasn't an option for him. Because he was the only child of Richard and Eliza Brennington, and so once he manifested the gifting, his career path was chosen for him. No questions. No options.

Eli had never let on that he didn't want to be a luminator. Not to his parents, Ronan, or Cassie. As much as he talked up going against his parents' wishes, he knew that their patience had its limits, and he made sure never to push past them. He could befriend Cassie and Ronan or pull small pranks at the many Brennington parties, and his parents would roll their eyes and write his actions off as annoying teenage antics. But if he ever tried to choose a different career, they'd disown him without a second thought. It wasn't worth the cost.

He'd never told Ronan the truth because Ronan would simply not be able to comprehend his lack of interest in lumination, and Eli knew he would resent him for it. Eli's family connections freely gave him everything that Ronan had to fight so hard to achieve. Eli could tell that Ronan had to work at not resenting him for the privilege as it was; it might push him over the edge if he knew that Eli didn't even want it.

And Cassie, well, he could just add this to the list of things he couldn't seem to tell her lately. Even though she'd never admit it, Eli thought Cassie had a special respect for luminators. He was worried that if she knew he didn't want to be one, it would diminish him in her eyes. That was the last thing he wanted.

So he kept his true desires to himself, continued on the path everyone expected him to be on, and treasured days like today when he could pour himself into what he truly loved. This work also helped to distract him from the fact that he'd barely talked to Cassie since they'd gone caving. He found himself checking his phone an embarrassing amount of times in the last few weeks.

He sat down again and pulled the book and dictionary back toward him. The translation was slow going and strange. From what he had deciphered, this was some kind of textbook or manual about lumination. At first, he thought it had to be hundreds of years old because it was written in Classical Gaelic, but the paper and ink were far too new and in too good a condition. He'd also found random words that were from a much later version of the language. He was beginning to suspect that the book was actually modern, or at least written sometime in the past hundred years, and the author had decided to write it in Classical Gaelic for reasons Eli couldn't begin to guess.

The later sections of the manual that he was working on now were even more difficult because he couldn't find some of the words in any of their dictionaries. Eli glanced at his phone, trying to convince himself that it was only to check the time and not also to see if he had any new texts from Cassie. He didn't have to be at his apprenticeship until tomorrow afternoon, so technically, he could swing an all-nighter, take a long nap in the morning, and still make it to the office on time and somewhat rested. He rang the maid for another strong cup of coffee. Long-lost words were no match for his caffeinated mind, the island's best-kept library, and an uninterrupted night of work.

———

THIS CAN'T BE REAL, Eli thought as he put his pen down hours later. He double-checked all of his work, looking up each archaic word again, and re-reading everything he'd written. Then he looked down at the last page of the manual one more time, making sure that he hadn't imagined the small drawing of the family crest in the corner.

He heard the large grandfather clock chiming in the foyer. 8:00 a.m. He pulled out his phone and texted Ronan and Cassie, all thoughts of a nap forgotten.

Meet me in half an hour. The usual place. It's important.

———

"HAVE YOU BEEN UP ALL NIGHT?" Ronan asked as he approached Eli, taking in his disheveled appearance—the wrinkled clothes, unkempt hair, and bloodshot eyes.

"I got wrapped up in this," Eli said, raising the leather-bound book. Ronan could see that his hands were shaking slightly. "God, where is Cassie? Why is she always late?" Eli started pacing back and forth.

"How much caffeine have you had in the past twelve hours?" Ronan asked.

"Trust me—it's not the caffeine that's making me act like this," Eli said, continuing to wear a path in the sand.

"What's going on, Eli?" Ronan asked.

"Finally," Eli said, as Cassie's car pulled into the car park nearby. "Let's wait for Cass—I don't want to have to explain this twice."

"Sorry it took me a while to get here," Cassie said as she joined them on the beach a moment later. "I was trying to convince Adele to come with me.

Things have been a little...complicated. Sorry I've been so MIA. Today I told her I had to come since your text sounded urgent. But that combined with these crazy headaches I keep having..."

Cassie trailed off when she noticed Eli glaring at her impatiently.

"You look terrible," Cassie told him.

"Okay, now that everyone is done talking," Eli began, ignoring Cassie's comment. "I want you both to hear me out. I've been working on translating this book for a while now. I'm not an expert, and I'm not saying I didn't make any mistakes, but at this point, I'm pretty sure what I have is more or less accurate. This is a manual about lumination, written sometime in the past hundred years, even though it's in Classical Gaelic—which is a really old language that hasn't been used in forever. That's weird enough by itself, but it's nothing compared to the final pages."

He paused and took a deep breath.

"They describe, in detail, how to destroy a memory."

"What are you talking about?" Ronan asked.

"Extinguish, annihilate, drain, eliminate. Take your pick. The end of the book shows how a luminator can kill a memory instead of revive it," Eli said.

Ronan couldn't keep the sarcasm out of his voice. "Eli, you dragged us out here to tell us that some crazy person wrote a book about something that no one can do?"

"I'm not convinced the author was crazy," Eli said, bristling at Ronan's dismissal.

"It has to be some kind of joke," Ronan replied, trying for a more even tone. "I mean, that's not possible. Cassie, help me out here." Ronan turned to Cassie, but she was just staring down at the sand, her expression pained.

"There is so much detail in here, like you would not believe," Eli went on. "Why would someone go to all of that trouble—even writing it down in a dead language—for a joke?"

"I don't know, people do all sorts of weird things," Ronan said. "There's no way this is real, Eli. It goes against the most basic tenets of our trade."

"What if everyone didn't believe in those tenets? Remember where we found this manual? Remember the humming sound? I think whoever wrote this was practicing it in the cave. It would make sense that they wouldn't want to do it in one of the offices where they might be discovered. That cavern was definitely large enough to house a mindscape, and no one would hear the noise from way out there. I know roughly where that part of the family land is, and no one lives near there."

"And how would this rogue luminator have hidden his actions during his closed memory session?"

"I don't know, Ronan!" Eli said. "I don't have all the answers, and I get that all of this could just be something some crazy person made up out of thin air. But, here's the hang up, what if it's not? What if this was real? What if someone was—or maybe still is—destroying other people's memories, and we stumbled onto proof about it and didn't do anything? I don't think I could live with myself if we found out somewhere down the line that this was actually happening, and we didn't take any action."

There was a beat of silence as Ronan considered his words.

"Cassie, what do you think? You haven't said anything." Eli asked, reaching out to brush her arm with his knuckles, a familiar jolt running through him as he did so.

She started at his touch. "What? Oh, sorry. Just getting another bad headache. Um, I think you should take it to the Council. If something like this is happening, then the Council will figure out how to stop it."

"You're actually entertaining the idea that this is real?" Ronan asked, the skepticism clear in his voice.

"No, I don't think it is," she said hesitantly. "But, I don't see the harm in making sure."

"Okay, so that's what I thought, about taking it to the Council. But then, I saw this," Eli said, opening the book to the last page and pointing to the bottom right hand corner. There was a small drawing of two falcons on either side of a shield marked with a large X.

It was the Roscoe family crest.

13

"I don't know what the Council will do with this," Eli said. "If this is real, and the Roscoes are involved, then it puts the Council's goal of protecting the profession directly at odds with their loyalty to the old families. I need to have more concrete proof, something they can't easily cover up, before I say anything about this."

Ronan stared at the page. Anyone could have drawn that crest. The Roscoe name was very well-known on Islayne, and anyone could have written that book. And yet, as Ronan looked at the drawing, he remembered Ben's face when he'd brought up his family. Was it possible that Ben knew...that he was somehow involved with this?

No. Ronan had never met anyone who loved lumination more than Ben Roscoe. There was no way he could be wrapped up in something like this. Destroying memories? That just wasn't possible. But then again, his trainer was the most skilled luminator Ronan had ever met. If anyone could discover a whole different facet of the gifting, it would be him. Ronan hadn't known him very long. Maybe he hadn't always loved the profession like he did now. Who knows what he'd been like fifteen years ago, when he was younger and more ambitious? Maybe then, when he'd had the falling out with his family, maybe then...

"It could still be nothing," Ronan said, hearing his own lack of conviction.

Cassie touched his back lightly. "Of course it could be," she said, a note of sympathy in her voice. "This doesn't prove anything."

"I'm not saying that anyone in the Roscoe family, or anyone else on the island, is involved. I'm not saying that it's even possible to destroy memories. I just think we should find out."

Eli looked between Ronan and Cassie, waiting.

Ronan realized that he didn't have a choice. Now that this seed of doubt had been planted in his mind, he wouldn't be able to root it out of his head until he knew for sure. He nodded at Eli.

"Okay. So how do we do that?" Cassie asked.

Eli smiled slightly, obviously relieved to be taken seriously. "I think I have an idea."

ONE WEEK LATER, Cassie pulled at the collar of her server uniform as the catering manager droned on about their responsibilities for the evening.

"Don't these shirts smell weird to you?" she whispered to Ronan as they stood in the back of the room. "And what are they made of? They are so itchy."

"Shh," he replied. "Pay attention. You're going to make us stand out."

The manager finally finished going over their responsibilities for the evening, and he told the room full of waiters and waitresses that they had fifteen minutes before they needed to report to the kitchen to get their serving trays.

Cassie and Ronan lagged behind the rest of the servers, making their way as slowly as possible down the expansive, ornate hallway of the Roscoe mansion, their footsteps not making a sound on the plush red carpet.

"God, that was tedious," Cassie said. "How hard can it be to walk around a bunch of rich people and offer them starters?"

"You do know that you're rich, right Cass?" Ronan asked.

"Not like this I'm not. My dad's money hasn't been sitting in a family vault for centuries."

Ronan gave her a pointed look.

"Okay, okay. Yes, that made me sound like a complete brat. I know I'm rich. I'm just annoyed that we have to do this tonight. I mean, why couldn't Eli have just gotten all of us invited to this party?"

"You're asking why he couldn't swing invitations to the Roscoes' party for two people that the old families unanimously hate?"

"We could have blended in," she mumbled.

"This is the only way we blend in," Ronan said, gesturing to their uniforms. "Eli was right. No one here will notice us as servers. But you know there's no way we could have been subtle party guests."

"It's just not fair. Adele gets to come as Eli's…I mean, they both get to come as guests and enjoy the party while we have to work."

Ronan noticed the color rising in Cassie's cheeks. He tried to hide his surprise. In all the time that he'd known Cassie, he'd never seen her jealous before, especially not when it came to Eli. Then again, Eli had never taken another girl on a date until now. Even if that date was with Adele, and even if it was just a cover so that they could try to find any more evidence about memory murder—as they'd taken to calling it—in the Roscoe mansion. Apparently, that was too much of a date for Cassie's liking.

"Well, if it makes you feel better," Ronan began, choosing his words carefully. "Eli told me he wished he could switch places with me. You know these kind of parties aren't really his thing."

Cassie brightened a bit at that. "Yeah, well, who could blame him? This will probably be such a dull evening. I feel bad for him."

Ronan decided not to point out that two minutes ago, Cassie had been upset about not being allowed to attend the terribly boring party whose guests she now pitied. They finally made it to the large kitchen where long tables were loaded with silver starter trays. Ronan's stomach growled at the delicious smells, and he realized he'd forgotten to eat before he came. He picked up a tray full of chicken liver pâté on toasted French baguette slices, choosing the dish that looked least appetizing so he wouldn't be constantly reminded of his hunger. Cassie picked up a tray of grilled shrimp drizzled with some kind of white sauce, and they followed the queue of servers back into a different corridor, and then finally out into the great hall.

As they stepped through the small side doors, Ronan had to keep himself from gasping. Barring the luminator workrooms, he was standing in the largest space he'd ever seen. The massive, curved ceiling far above his head looked like it was made up of all glass, each immense panel detailing a complicated pattern of dazzling colors, and in the center hung a glowing, ornate chandelier. On the far side of the room, two identical curved staircases flowed down from the walkways on the second story. Large, carved marble columns and high arches jutted out about ten feet from the walls on the main floor, creating small alcoves all around the edges of the room. The dark wood floor gleamed, reflecting the lights of the column sconces and the chandelier. Ronan thought back to the first time he'd seen Ben's cluttered, dirty office. What could make someone want to leave a place like this to live in a place like that?

"Okay, now I don't even feel bad saying it. I am *not* rich like this," Cassie said as she craned her neck to look up at the ceiling.

They spent the next hour walking around the great hall, offering starters to the slowly-growing crowd of guests. At promptly 8:00 p.m., Richard and Eliza Brennington arrived, followed closely behind by Eli and Adele. Ronan caught his breath as he saw Adele walking down the staircase. She looked stunning. Her hair was pulled up in a complicated bun, and she wore a long, flowing blue dress that looked to be shifting shades as it caught the different lights in the room. Eli turned to say something to her as they reached the main floor, and she laughed in response, her whole face lighting up. Ronan felt a twinge of jealousy at how happy Adele looked on Eli's arm. He knew that Eli wasn't interested in her, but as usual, he had no idea what was going on in her mind.

Ronan realized his tray was almost empty and started to make his way back to the kitchen. He'd just walked behind one of the pillars when a voice on the other side of it pulled him up short.

"Did you see the rack on Brennington's date? God, I could show her a good time. Eli wouldn't know where to start with a girl like that. Mmhmm if I could get the chance to get her off by herself tonight. She looks like the type who'd say no, but only at first..."

Ronan would know Kendrick's voice anywhere. He could hear the blood pounding in his ears. He turned back, ready to step around the pillar and hit Kendrick upside the head with the heavy serving tray. But he stopped himself and started walking back toward the kitchen before he overheard anymore of the conversation and completely lost all self-control.

Pausing back by the smaller doors the servers were supposed to use, Ronan took a couple of deep breaths and tried to calm down. He could not lose his cool right now. They might not get another chance to be here for months—the Roscoes didn't throw parties like this every weekend. He had to stick to the plan. He was supposed to wait two more hours, until most of the guests had consumed a lot more alcohol, and then he and Cassie would slip away and search through the library, and Eli and Adele would do the same thing in the study. Ronan could not draw attention to himself and risk getting kicked out of the party. Kendrick was an ass, but Adele was smart, and besides, she was going to be with Eli all evening anyway.

Ronan pushed through the doors and retrieved more food from the kitchen. When he came back a few minutes later, Cassie caught sight of him by the side entrance and weaved her way through the crowd until she was standing next to him. "Are you okay?" she asked. "I saw you walk out a few minutes ago, and you looked like you were about ready to kill someone."

"Pretty much. I overheard Kendrick talking about Adele."

"What did he say?" she asked, her eyes narrowing.

"It's not important. Just him being a dick. I'm okay now. I've calmed down..." He trailed off as he caught sight of Adele across the room, talking animatedly with Kendrick.

"Ronan?" Cassie asked.

"New plan. Adele and I are going to search the library now," Ronan said, striding across the room.

"Ronan! What are you doing?" Cassie hissed as he walked away, but Ronan pretended not to hear her.

"Can I offer you some smoked salmon?" he asked as he approached Adele and Kendrick. He tried his best to disguise his voice, and he kept his eyes down. Then he tripped on purpose, and his serving tray knocked into Adele's full glass of champagne, spilling the light liquid all down the front of her dress.

She cried out and jumped back in surprise.

"You idiot!" Kendrick yelled at him.

"Oh, I'm sorry. I'm so clumsy," Ronan said, not looking up at Kendrick, and positioning himself between the two of them. "Here, if you come with me, I'm sure I can find someone to get that stain out." He hurried Adele toward the back of the room, leaving a fuming Kendrick alone in the middle of the floor.

"What the hell was that?!" she whispered angrily. "Do you have any idea how expensive this dress was?"

"Trust me, Eli won't miss the funds," Ronan said. "There's been a change of plans. We need to go search the library now."

"Why now? And why not with Eli?" she asked.

Ronan felt another twinge of jealousy. Was she disappointed to be stuck with him? "I'll explain it to you when we get there."

They left the great hall. Thanks to Eli, they knew exactly how to get to the library. Apparently, this wasn't the first time he'd snuck out of one of the Roscoes' parties to go exploring their mansion, though it would be the first time with such a specific purpose in mind. They walked silently through three different hallways and down one staircase before arriving at the intricately-carved doors of the library a few minutes later. Ronan pushed open the doors, and they both rushed inside. He breathed a sigh of relief when it was clear no one else was in the room. Adele turned to face him.

"So why the change in plans, and why exactly did you need to ruin the one ball gown I've ever worn in my life?"

"That guy you were talking to, Kendrick, he's…not a nice guy."

She waited for him to continue, her expression unreadable.

"I'd overheard him talking about you before, stuff you wouldn't have liked. And then I saw that you were standing with him, and obviously you didn't know what a total jerk he was so, I just…" Ronan trailed off at the look on Adele's face.

"That's why you made me spill my drink and completely changed the plan for tonight?" she asked, her voice dangerously low and even. "Because I was talking to a guy that you don't like? God, Ronan! You don't have to protect me. I'm not some idiot girl who falls for the first guy who gives her a compliment. I know who Kendrick is—Eli told me on the way over here—and I could tell within thirty seconds of talking to him that he was a jerk. But I was trying to get information from him. He's a Lydon. I was trying to figure out if he knew anything. But now, I'll never get the chance because you didn't trust me. And you risked him recognizing you!"

"I knew he probably wouldn't. Guys like him don't ever look twice at servers."

"That's not the point!"

"I know, I know. I'm sorry," Ronan said, holding up his hands. "Okay? I shouldn't have done that. It's just...when I saw you two together, after what I'd heard him say, I wasn't thinking straight. I couldn't stand him talking to you."

"Why do you care anyways?" she asked.

"Because I—" Ronan paused, not sure how to proceed. "I...hate that guy. And you deserve better."

She sighed. "I wasn't angling for a ring. I was just trying to get some information."

"I know. You're right. I should have realized you would see through someone like him."

"What did he say that made you so mad?" she asked.

"Well, he, might have mentioned something about your...body, and, uh, getting you alone tonight. The specifics aren't important."

"They seem to be important enough to make you blush."

"I'm not blushing!" Ronan protested, feeling the heat rise in his face.

She sighed again and seemed to let go of her frustration, or at least redirect it away from Ronan.

"I can't do anything about him right now," she said. "Since we're here, we might as well look around."

They starting combing through the shelves of the library, looking for anything remotely related to memory murder. Eli had written out all the comparable words in Classical Gaelic and had given them each a copy in case they found anything that looked similar.

After a few minutes of stony silence, Adele started to warm up to him again and told Ronan about her first interaction with Eli's parents. She said his mother had managed to drop the Brennington name no less than five times within the first five minutes of their conversation. Ronan told her that was actually pretty low for Eliza.

Adele asked him about previous summer adventures with Eli and Cassie, and Ronan soon had her laughing about the time Cassie convinced him and Eli to streak through the massive gardens in front of the Lydons' summer cottage. They were caught by Kendrick's grandmother who, they discovered too late, was living there at the time.

"Okay, I need to take a break," Ronan said after an hour of fruitless searching. They sat down in the back corner of the library.

"I want to ask you something," Adele said. "And I don't want you to get mad about it."

"Okay," Ronan said. "I'll do my best."

"Why do you guys think it would be *so* terrible if someone was destroying memories? I mean, I get that it's not a good thing, especially if a luminator was doing it against a person's will, which is why I wanted to help with this. But still, it's not like they were murdering *people*."

Ronan tried to think how best to explain it to her. It was so apparent to him, it felt like trying to explain why water tasted good after walking in the sun or why it was necessary to breathe.

"When you manifest the luminator gifting," he began. "You don't just have the ability to revive memories, you also hone a kind of sense about them. In a session, it's easy to see that memories are dangerous and powerful, but it's also just as clear that they are inherently good and precious. Even painful memories. They are so intricately tied to a person's humanity. That is why our whole trade centers around reviving them, because in that way, we make life more real. We make people more human. For a luminator, who has spent countless hours in the presence of memories, the idea that he could somehow harm them is…unthinkable. It's revolting."

He shuddered involuntarily.

Adele stared at him for a moment. "I think it's cool," she said finally. "How much you love this stuff."

"It's worth loving," he said softly. Then he cleared his throat. "Uh, so, since we're all asking questions here, can I ask you one?"

"As long as it's not to streak down the hallway here, then yes."

"Why were you so upset when you came in to the bookstore the day we met?"

"Why were you acting so strange?" Adele countered.

"Our mutual favorite party guest had just ripped my future to shreds right in front of me, and I was contemplating a life of shelving bad-smelling books."

"Has anyone ever told you that you're a little dramatic?"

"Yes, mannnnny times," Ronan said, stretching his hands out in front of him theatrically. "But don't change the subject. I answered your question, now you have to answer mine."

"It's going to sound like the most cliché answer in the world."

"I think I can handle it."

"My parents have decided to separate, on a trial basis, or whatever."

"Oh...I'm so sorry. That might be common, Adele, but I don't think it's ever cliché."

"Well, I'm not sorry," she said fiercely. "They've been unhappy forever, and I think the only reason they've stayed together this long is for me. I barely ever see my dad anyways. He's always traveling for work. It won't even be that different."

"That's not why you were upset?" he asked.

She shook her head. "My mum and I are really close. Maybe it's because my dad is gone so much, or because I'm an only child. But whatever the reason, she's never really treated me like a kid. We've always been more like friends. She shares things with me. I knew that things were rough with my dad, but she never let on that it was this bad. And then, instead of talking to me about the trial separation and letting me stay to help her figure things out, I'm shipped off here for the summer, no questions asked. Like I'm a little kid who has to stay far away from any hint of divorce, like it's a disease I could catch."

Ronan didn't say anything for a moment. He wondered whether he should tell Adele what he was thinking. After all, she was finally talking to him, really talking. Not ignoring, not avoiding, and not just making small talk. Sitting in the back corner of the deserted library felt intimate, and he didn't want to ruin the moment. But then again, if he couldn't be honest with her, there was no point to this anyway.

"Well," he began slowly. "You're saying that you're mad that your mum is treating you like a kid instead of a peer. But I'm wondering if you're mad because she's not treating you like *her* kid."

"Shouldn't we find a couch somewhere so we do can this whole psychoanalysis thing properly?"

"She sent you away for the whole summer instead of letting you stay and helping *you* figure things out. She should be there for you right now, but she's not."

"What's to figure out? They'll probably get a divorce. It happens to couples all of the time."

"That doesn't make it any easier," Ronan said.

"How would you know?" Adele asked angrily. "How would you have any idea how I'm feeling?"

Ronan almost told her she was right, and he had no idea what he was talking about. But she hadn't said that he was wrong; she just got angry. Which made him think that he was right in what he was saying. And maybe if it was someone else, he would have let it go. But he found himself caring about Adele, and if she couldn't face the reason she was upset, nothing would change.

"You told me before that you think forgetting exists for a reason. I think you want to forget that your mum is still your mum, even if she's also your friend, and it's normal to feel angry if she's not acting like either one."

Adele didn't say anything for a moment. "Do you always tell strangers how they really feel about what's going on in their lives?" she asked finally.

"No," he said, turning toward her, their faces just inches apart. "But somehow you've never felt like a stranger."

She began to lean in closer to him, but then the library doors banged open. Even as Ronan jolted back in surprise, there was a part of him boiling over in frustration at being interrupted *again* at such a particularly opportune moment with Adele. He looked around frantically, but then realized there was probably no better place to hide than where they were already sitting, with several rows of bookshelves sheltering them from the front of the room.

"Who are you? Let go of me!" a male voice cried out.

"Jeremy, please calm down. This is not the time or the place for one of your meltdowns. Where is that useless nurse aide?"

Ronan recognized the second voice. It belonged to Diane Roscoe, Ben's mother. He was sure of it because she had a very distinct voice—low and gravelly—that she'd used to turn down his offer of champagne two hours ago. Ronan knew that Ben had a brother about eight years younger than him named Jeremy, but Ronan had no idea if he was the other person in the room since Ronan had never met him. The Roscoes enrolled their second son at some fancy year-round boarding school in England soon after Ben cut ties with his family. Ronan remembered his own mom—who rarely cared or commented on the actions of the old Islayne families—saying how strange and sad it was that the Roscoes would lose one son, and then so soon after, send the other one hundreds of miles away.

"Why are you talking to me like you know who I am?" Jeremy asked, sounding shaken.

Diane sighed. "I do know who you are, dear," she said, a tender note replacing her earlier frustration.

"Well I don't know *you*, or this place, or, or, who I am. What is that screaming?" Jeremy asked, his voice rising.

"It's not real. It's okay. I know you're confused, Jeremy, but everything will be okay soon, I promise. Just please try to calm down."

They heard the door open again.

"There you are!" Diane said. "Where the hell have you been? I found him wandering the halls *alone.*"

"I am so sorry, ma'am," came a third voice, also male. "I stepped out for a moment. I needed to take a call. He was calm, sleeping, when I left. I promise."

"We don't pay you to make phone calls during work hours. You can tell me your excuses later," Diane said. "Right now, you must get him to calm down. I can't stand seeing him like this. And we have *guests*."

Ronan tensed, thinking that Diane had seen them. But then he realized she was referring to the mass of people in the great hall.

"Stop talking about me like I'm not here! You can't keep me against my will!" Jeremy cried.

"No, no, of course not. Here, Jeremy, please come with me, and I promise I will explain everything to you," the aide said.

The doors opened and closed again. No sound came from the front of the room. Ronan couldn't be sure that everyone had left, but he didn't want to stay crouched in the corner of the library all night either. After a few moments, he got Adele's attention, pointed to himself, and inclined his head in the direction of the library doors. He motioned for her to stay where she was. Then he slowly stood up and crept around the nearest bookshelf to get a better view of the front of the room. He saw Diane Roscoe standing as still as a statue, staring at the ornate doors. At nearly six feet tall with a severe face and sharp eyes, she was a formidable-looking woman. But at the moment, her shoulders were slouched forward, as if the previous few minutes had taken some of the steel out of her spine. She clenched her hands tightly into fists. Finally, she took a deep breath, stood tall, and strode purposefully out of the room.

14

"What do you mean they already left for the library?" Eli asked. "That wasn't the plan! How could Ronan be so stupid? Kendrick could have recognized him!"

"I'd say it was a mixture of male bravado and good intentions," Cassie said.

Eli shook his head in frustration. They stood back in the corner of the great hall, blocked from the view of most of the guests by one of the pillars. "Okay, well, nothing for it but to go search the study now. There's a higher chance they'll get caught being in the library this early in the evening. Might as well try to get in as much time as possible before that happens."

Cassie almost had to run to keep pace with Eli as he burst out into the hallway.

"Slow down!" Cassie whispered urgently. "You're going to draw more attention to us if you start sprinting toward the study."

Eli checked his pace.

"Thank you," she said. "You know it took me a good hour to get you alone in there to tell you what had happened. You are very popular at these things."

"No, actually, my parents are popular at these things. People just see me as an easy way to get a good word in with them."

"Well, this is awkward," Cassie said teasingly. "Because I was planning on using tonight to confess to you my true intentions for being your friend in the first place."

Eli didn't respond.

"I was just kidding," she said.

He sighed. "Sorry, I know you're joking. It's just these parties. They get under my skin. I'm tired of everyone looking at me and calculating what they can get in return for being polite to me."

"I didn't know they grated on you so much. You don't talk about it."

"It comes with the territory," Eli said, shrugging. "No use complaining about it. But for some reason, it was getting to me more tonight."

"You looked like you were having an okay time, at least when I saw you come in with Adele," Cassie said, the slightest edge to her voice.

"Yeah, well, Adele was great. But maybe that was the problem. I had to go from talking with her, where she treated me like a person, to talking to all my parents' sycophants."

Cassie tugged at her uniform again, suddenly very aware of the unflattering cut of the white blouse. The image of Adele looking flawless on Eli's arm rose unbidden in her mind. Cassie ignored the slight tightening in her chest at Eli's enthusiasm over his time with Adele.

Stop being ridiculous, she told herself. *They are friends. Of course he likes spending time with her. I love spending time with her. It just means he has good taste in people. And besides, why should I care either way?*

They reached the study moments later. A large window took up almost one whole side of the room. On the far wall was a white stone fireplace with a large high-backed armchair in front of it. Across from that stood a massive, dark wooden desk. A small chandelier hung down in the center of the room. *What is with these people and their chandeliers?* Cassie wondered. *Did they have a ton of stock in a lighting company?*

"There is a lot less storage in here than I remember from last time," Eli said, looking around the room. "Sorry, this might be a dead end."

Cassie shrugged. "Let's find out."

They began combing through the large desk. "You're looking better tonight," Eli remarked. "Are those headaches gone?"

"Yeah," she said. "First time in while that my mind feels clear." She stood up for a moment and stretched her arms behind her back. "Whew. This beats walking around offering people food all evening. Though I would have killer biceps if I kept it up. Those trays are freaking heavy."

"I'm glad it was just for tonight, then," Eli said as he leafed through a mess of paper on top of the desk. "You already have nice arms."

Cassie paused in her search of the desk drawers, not sure how to react to his words. Eli didn't make a habit of complimenting any part of her body.

"You're just worried that you'd lose to me in arm-wrestling if I took up professional catering," she said finally.

He shrugged. "It's a moot point because you could never do that for a living. All the polite smiles and nodding and calling people sir and ma'am—you wouldn't stand a week of that. I'm surprised you lasted for as long as you did tonight."

"You'd be amazed at how well I can fake it for a good cause."

"Then you should have been in Adele's place tonight. She almost burst out laughing when one of last year's Council appointees found four different ways to compliment my suit."

"I would have," Cassie said, slamming the desk drawer harder than she'd intended and standing up. "But you didn't ask me."

Cassie cringed inwardly at the hurt tone in her voice. She hadn't meant to say that so harshly. Why was she so short-tempered tonight? If anything, she should be less irritable since the headaches that had been plaguing her on and off since they explored the cavern had finally let up for the evening.

Eli stopped rummaging through a pile of letters and walked over to her. He leaned back against the side of the desk, looking at her intently.

"You know people would have recognized you as my date, Cass. My parents aren't the only well-known ones around here."

"I know, I know," she said airily. "I was only joking."

"But I would've, I mean I wanted to take you, if things were different."

"Sure," she said, suddenly feeling like the room had shrunk in size. "Because...I, I could've kept a straight face, when that guy started fawning over you."

They both heard the click of the doorknob turning. She looked around, panicked that they were about to get caught, but there was nowhere to hide.

"Don't freak out," he whispered. Then as the door swung open, he did the last thing she'd expected under the circumstances. He took her hands, pulled her into his arms, and started kissing her. She could smell the expensive aftershave on his face, and his lips felt cool and refreshing against hers. Her mind was still trying to process what was happening when a voice cut in.

"Slumming it with the hired help?" Adele asked. "Very classy."

Cassie broke off the kiss and jumped back from Eli. She stared at Ronan and Adele as they walked in and shut the door behind them, at a loss for how to explain what had just happened. She also felt irrationally hurt by Adele's comment, even though she knew she was joking.

"Sorry guys," Eli said, sounding completely at ease. "That was the simplest excuse I could think of for why Cassie and I would be in here in case someone else was walking through that door."

Cassie glanced back at Eli. He looked calm and composed. She finally found her voice.

"You could have told me you were going to do that!"

"There wasn't exactly time to debate the pros and cons of the decision," he responded in the same nonchalant voice.

Ridiculously, Cassie felt tears pricking the corners of her eyes. She didn't know why Eli's reaction bothered her so much. Anger roiled around in her stomach. She took a deep breath and tried to calm herself down. She was *not* going to cry right now.

"Can you guys fight about this later?" Ronan asked, clearly irritated. "Unlike you, we were actually taking this night seriously and trying to find proof and—"

"*You* were the one who changed the plan and almost got caught because of your stupid vendetta against Kendrick," Cassie cut Ronan off, happy to have a clearer target for her anger. "Don't talk to me about taking this night seriously!"

"Can everyone lower their voices?" Adele asked, glancing toward the door. "A shouting match might not be the best way to keep people from noticing us. We really do need to talk to you guys about what we found, or actually, heard."

Once everyone had calmed down, Adele told Eli and Cassie about the conversation in the library.

"I think this guy, Jeremy, could be the proof we need," Eli said excitedly after Adele finished talking. Cassie couldn't help but notice that this news seemed to have a bigger effect on him than kissing her.

"In the manual, it describes how the destroyed memories leave a kind of residue in the mind," he continued. "If we could find a luminator to do a session with Jeremy, then we could know for sure whether any of his memories have been destroyed. There's no way the Council could hide something that concrete."

"Wait—we don't even know for sure if this is proof of anything," Ronan said. "He could just have dementia or something."

"I don't know. He sounded pretty young," Adele said. "I'd say early-twenties tops."

"People can get it young," Ronan said. "Or there could be another explanation. We still don't even know if this memory murder thing is *real*."

"That's why I'm saying we should figure out a way to have a session done and—"

"How?" Ronan cut Eli off. "Are you suggesting we search through the rest of the mansion until we find this guy—which could take forever, especially since none of us knows what he looks like—and then what, kidnap him? Knock him out and hope no one from the party notices us carrying an unconscious man through the hallways? And did you have a luminator in mind who would perform a session without pay on the word of a few kids with a halfway translated-book that may or may not be accurate?"

"I'm getting the sense you hope it's the latter," Eli said.

"Of course I do! This is our profession, Eli. This is the only thing I want to do with my life! Of course I don't want this to be real."

"So we shouldn't do anything?" Eli asked, his voice rising to match Ronan's. "We should just bury our heads in the sand? Whether you want it to be real or not, we have an obligation to try to find out!"

"Again with the yelling," Adele said. "God, what is with everyone tonight? Okay, we are obviously not going to come to a decision immediately. I think we should just leave the party now and regroup tomorrow. Is that okay with everyone?"

Eventually, they all agreed and filed out of the study. Adele and Eli were going back to the great hall, but Eli showed Cassie and Ronan the nearest exit since they'd both had enough serving for one night. As Cassie and Ronan were about to leave, they realized that both of their mobile phones were still in the back of the kitchen. The catering manager had threatened them on pain of death to leave their phones in the kitchen while they served.

After managing to sneak into the back and retrieve their phones, they headed for the exit Eli had showed them. Suddenly, Ronan pulled Cassie off to the side in a small alcove, and he inclined his head to where they had been walking. Cassie could see hurt and confusion in his expression. She looked over to see Adele giggling and pulling Kendrick by the hand to a darkened corner of the hallway. She watched, stunned, as Adele backed up against the wall and Kendrick leaned in close to her. Then suddenly, Adele brought her knee up swift and hard into his groin. She stepped around him as he doubled over in pain.

"You're right—you *do* know how to show a girl a good time," she said over her shoulder as she walked back into the great hall.

15

"No, that's not even close," Ben said, slamming the book shut and then getting up to put it away in his office. He came back a moment later and sat down in the chair across from Ronan, leaning back in it and peering down at him.

"The official term for the mindscape is called the *lusita*," he said. "Did you even read this chapter?"

"Why does it even matter if I know the official name?" Ronan asked. "I can do the work. That's all that matters."

"Except that you'll never get the chance to do the work if you don't pass the examination and receive your full license."

"So now you actually care about me practicing? I'm not just here to keep your rooms clean?"

"If you don't know the answer to that by now, I don't think my words are going to make a difference. Are you going to tell me why you can't seem to concentrate on anything today or would you prefer to just continue to mope around my office?"

Ben wasn't exactly right. Ronan was focused—just not on the technical terms of lumination. He couldn't stop thinking about the party last night. Was Jeremy truly proof of memory elimination? And if so, how many other victims were there? And was the man sitting across from Ronan—a man that he had come to respect if not always enjoy—wrapped up in it? Is that why he'd had a falling out with his family?

The questions kept spinning around in his mind. Each time he thought of Jeremy's voice—the fear, the confusion, the anger—Ronan got a sick feeling in the pit of his stomach. Was he learning from a man who could do something like that to another human being? Could Ben ever have robbed another person of his memories? Could he ever have stripped away such an integral piece of someone's humanity?

No. Ronan refused to believe it. There was still so little proof, and there were much more probable explanations for Jeremy's condition. Anyone could have drawn that crest, and anyone could have made up the stuff in that manual. Ben had done nothing to warrant Ronan's distrust.

But Ronan suspected that he would be alone in that conclusion when he met up with Eli, Cassie, and Adele tonight to talk about what they should do. Maybe if he could find a way to ask Ben about it without raising his suspicions, he could have more to back up his opinion.

"I'm not moping," Ronan answered. "Sorry, I'm just tired. I had a late night last night. Remember you told me to have more of a social life?"

"Yes, well, that was supposed to make you more agreeable, not less," Ben said.

"I'll work on that," Ronan answered. "And I promise I will go back and study that chapter until my eyes bleed. But before I do, can I ask you something?"

Ben inclined his head slightly.

"I've been thinking, with all the textbooks we have on lumination, do you think that's all there is to know?"

Ben's eyes narrowed. "Considering that you haven't even begun to master the amount of information we do have, are you really keen on there being more?"

Ronan shrugged. "It was just a random thought I had—that maybe there was some part of lumination, some facet of the gifting that hadn't been discovered yet."

Ben considered Ronan for a moment, his face unreadable. "If you have so much time to be entertaining these kind of thoughts while you're here," he said finally. "Then maybe I'm not giving you enough work to occupy your mind. I want you to read the next six chapters of that textbook by tomorrow. And if you answer any of my questions wrong, then you won't be allowed to join in on sessions with Jillian for the rest of this week."

"That's not fair! I can't possibly read and remember that much information in half a day!"

"Perhaps you should have considered the limits of your abilities before running your mouth about things beyond your comprehension!"

"It was just a question!"

"You have been given a specific gifting for a specific purpose," Ben said, his eyes glinting dangerously. "It's not a toy to be tinkered with in your free time. You have a responsibility to the world to master this craft and to use it to enrich the lives of other people. If that bores you, if what I'm trying to teach you isn't enough, then you can walk out that door and never come back here again."

Ronan held up his hands. "No, no, listen I'm sorry. I won't ever bring it up again. This is enough for me, this is all that I want to do with my gifting. I promise."

Ben nodded slightly and stood up. "I'm going to get some lunch. Start reading those chapters."

After he left, Ronan realized that his trainer had never answered his question.

CASSIE KNOCKED on Eli's front door. One of the Brennington's many ever-changing maids—the same ones never managed to stay hired for long—opened it.

"Hi. Um, I'm here to see Eli," Cassie said. She never quite knew how to interact with their maids. She felt like she should introduce herself and ask how they were doing, but when she tried, the maids looked at her like she was breaking some kind of unspoken social order. But if she didn't say anything, or jumped right to what she was there for, then she felt like a jerk.

Her father was pretty rich now, and they did have a cleaning service come once a week, but that was different. Those people weren't servants; they were just doing a job. Employing a maid felt like something out of a previous century. Even the Roscoes and the Lydons hired cleaning and gardening companies in lieu of servants, but the Brenningtons obviously had no issue with the concept.

The maid nodded silently and led her up one the curved staircases that framed either side of the large foyer. Cassie lived in a beautiful home. She knew that. But there was something intangible about the Brennington mansion that made her home feel cheap by comparison. Eli once told her it was because his parents' pretension tended to rub off on everything around them, including their home. Cassie had often felt that only Eli was immune to it.

She searched her mind for something appropriate and yet friendly to say as they walked down the long, spacious hallway, and she was still searching as the unnamed maid knocked on and then opened Eli's door, announced that Cassie was here to see him, and left without another word.

Cassie stepped inside. Per usual, Eli's clothes and books were strewn haphazardly around the room, but Cassie was glad of it. His clutter made the large room feel lived-in and comfortable, unlike the austere beauty of the rest of the mansion. Normally, Eli's room was the only place in the Brennington's home where Cassie felt like she could relax without fear of dirtying or breaking something. But tonight, being alone with Eli made her think of what happened the last time they were alone, less than twenty-four hours ago, so she wasn't relaxed either way.

Though she'd been friends with Eli for years, the sight of Adele on his arm the night before had triggered something in Cassie. She hadn't known until yesterday how much she hated the idea of Eli going on a date with anyone else. That thought, combined with her hurt and frustration over his complete lack of response after kissing her, had been distracting her all day. But she wasn't quite ready to deal with the implications of how she was feeling.

"I guess I'm the first one here?" Cassie asked

"Yeah," Eli said, looking up from the papers on his desk. "Ronan just texted me and said he's running late. Where's Adele?"

"Her mum called when we were getting ready to leave. Adele told me she'd just ride my bike over when she was done talking to her."

Cassie perched on the edge of his bed and tried to look at ease.

"Hey, I'm actually glad we have a few minutes alone. I've been meaning to talk to you, about what happened last night."

"What's to talk about?" Cassie asked.

"About the kiss. I—"

"Oh no, no. You seemed to have it all figured out. It was the perfect excuse. As you explained so rationally last night."

"Well, you have to admit, it kind of was, but –"

"So good," she said, feeling herself getting angry again. "We're agreed!"

"Would you stop interrupting? I'm trying to tell you that I shouldn't have done that without talking to you first."

"Who cares? It's not like it meant anything anyways. How did Adele put it, 'slumming with the hired help?' That sounds about right. I mean, I definitely wasn't the one wearing an expensive ball gown and charming your parents last night."

"What does that have to do with anything? I thought we agreed that I couldn't have asked you last night."

"Yes. You've very *logically* explained all of your recent decisions. So like I said, there's nothing we need to talk about."

"Then why are you so upset?" Eli asked.

"Well I figure one of us should show some sort of emotion! You obviously weren't affected by the kiss at all. You're like a freaking robot."

"And you're saying that you were?"

"I was what?"

"Affected? By the kiss?" Eli asked, standing up from his desk.

"What? No, I didn't, I mean that's not what I said...."

He walked over to her. "Because that kiss was one of the best moments of my life," he said quietly. He was just inches away from her now. Cassie could smell the faint scent of his soap and mouthwash. She looked at him, taking in his disheveled blond hair and wide, dark eyes. Arguing with him felt so familiar. Everything about him felt known, comfortable, and safe. She'd shared so much with him over the past three years, and no one knew her like he did.

But in another way, this felt like entirely new territory. Because she'd never seen him look at her like that before. She thought of how his lips had felt against hers the previous night. As if he could read her thoughts, Eli started to lean in toward her.

"Wait," she said, putting her hands on his shoulders. "Wait please, I need to think about this." She stepped around him and walked over to his desk, taking a deep breath.

"What's to think about?" Eli asked.

"It's just a lot—you, me. It could change a lot of things."

"Things have already changed," he said.

"Not like this."

Eli let out his breath and ran his fingers distractedly through his hair. "So you're saying it's not worth the risk?"

"No, I'm saying what I said. This is all *really* new for me. I don't want to rush into anything."

"This would be the one time you want to be cautious," Eli said ruefully.

"Well, take that as a compliment. Maybe I've finally found something worth being cautious about. So give me some time, okay?"

The seconds stretched out between them.

"Okay, how about now?" Eli asked, but this time he was grinning. She shook her head in fake annoyance and sat down in Eli's chair. She leafed through the manual just to have something else to do with her hands. "So, have you translated any more of this?" she asked.

"Yeah, I'm almost done, but I just…"

His voice faded from Cassie's hearing as she looked at the front of the book again. Something pulled at her mind insistently, and the pounding at her temples came back in full force. Suddenly, an ear-piercing, otherworldly scream filled her head, and in her mind's eye, she saw a dim light reflected off a cavern wall, and then a woman laying on a metal table. Just as quickly, the sights and the sound vanished from her mind. She could hear Eli's voice calling to her as if from far away. She tried to stand up, but the pain roared through her head, overwhelming her senses and forcing her to her knees. Dark spots crowded into her vision. The last thing she remembered was the feel of Eli's hands on her arms. Then everything went dark.

16

"What do you mean, she just passed out?" Adele asked.

"She seemed fine one minute, and then the next thing I know, she was kneeling on my floor, looking like she was about to throw up, and then she just slumped over," Eli said, sounding frantic.

The voices felt like sandpaper grating against Cassie's eardrums. "Please stop talking so loudly," she groaned.

She opened her eyes to see Adele, Ronan, and Eli all looking down at her with almost identical worried expressions. At another time, she probably would have found it funny. But there was still a throbbing pain in her head, and it kept her normal sense of humor at bay.

"Cassie, are you okay?" Adele asked.

"I'm not sure. I feel awful, but at least I don't think I'm going to pass out again."

"What happened?" Eli asked.

"I don't know exactly," Cassie answered. "I was looking at that book, and it…triggered something in me. I heard this really loud, terrible scream, and I saw something. I can't remember now. Someone in the cavern, I think."

"A scream?" Eli asked. "That's…they mention that in the manual. The memory produces a scream when it's getting torn up. Do you think you'd been to that cavern before?"

"I think she would have remembered if she'd witnessed a luminator destroying someone else's memories in that cavern, Eli," Ronan said. "I don't think that's the kind of thing you forget."

"But maybe, if she'd been caught…"

"Then she wouldn't remember anything," Ronan said.

"Can you guys stop arguing please?" Cassie asked. "I need to go home and lie down."

"I'll drive you," Adele said, helping Cassie to her feet.

"I'll come check on you later, okay Cass?" Eli asked.

"Yeah, me too," Ronan echoed.

She tried nodding, but that sent more pain shooting through her head. She gave them a weak smile and then let Adele help her out the door.

EVEN THOUGH SHE WAS EXHAUSTED, Cassie's headache kept her awake for hours as she tossed and turned in her bed. Every so often, she would hear the scream, or see one of the two mental snapshots in her mind, but they never stayed for long. Cassie wondered briefly if this was what people felt like right before they went insane. Finally, she fell into a fitful sleep, only to wake up feeling just as exhausted as before. It was pitch black outside. Cassie reached over and checked her phone. 4 a.m. She laid back and stared up at the darkness, trying to will the pain out of her head. But when it became clear that the pain wasn't going to listen, she gave up and went downstairs. As Cassie made her way down the hall, the delicious smell of brewed coffee wafted out into the foyer. She entered the kitchen to see Adele sitting in one of the stools by the island, holding a steaming mug in both hands.

"Hey, fancy meeting you here," Adele said as she caught sight of Cassie.

"Couldn't sleep?" Cassie asked, pouring herself a cup and taking a seat next to her.

Adele shook her head.

"Join the club. We should make t-shirts."

"As long as they're bright neon, and the print is comic sans, I'm in." Adele held up her mug in a toast.

"Why couldn't you sleep?" Cassie asked.

"It happens to me a lot."

"Really? It never happens to me."

"Then I might have to kick you out of the club."

Cassie smiled slightly at that.

"Seriously though, how are you feeling?" Adele asked.

Cassie stared down at her mug. "I...I don't know. My head keeps pounding. Every so often, I see one of those weird, hazy scenes in my head or hear that awful screaming. It's so bizarre. And each time I think about it, I get this sick feeling in my stomach, like I ate something rotten. I don't know what's going on with me."

"Maybe your mind has, you know, suppressed something up until now. It'll probably come back in its own time."

"But what if it doesn't? I can't stay in this weird limbo forever. And these scenes, it's like, you know, when you have the answer to a question on the tip of your tongue, but it just won't come to you in the moment? More is there, in my mind, but I just can't access it. And it's the uncertainty that's killing me. If only I could recall more, I think it would help make sense of everything."

"I think you're just gonna have to be patient."

"I don't want to be patient! I want to know what these memories are, and I want to know now."

Adele put down her coffee cup and gave Cassie her most serious look.

"What?" Cassie asked.

"I know you like to throw out the rules and take crazy risks all the time. But you can't do what you're thinking of doing right now."

"I don't know what you're talking about."

"Stop playing dumb. I love you, Cassie, and I'll do whatever I can to help you work through this. But you are the one who told me that it's incredibly dangerous—not to mention illegal—for an apprentice to do a solo session. You can't ask Ronan or Eli to dig around in your head."

"I know I can't ask them. Besides, Ronan wouldn't do it in a million years. He'd be way too worried that he would mess up."

"You can't ask Eli, either."

"Adele, relax. I'm not going to ask either of them. I might be reckless sometimes, but I'm not stupid. That would be way too dangerous for everyone."

"Do you promise?" Adele asked, holding Cassie's gaze.

"Yes! I promise. Now can you stop lecturing me? It's been a long night already."

Adele nodded. "It'll be okay, Cassie. We'll find another way to figure all of this out."

Cassie just shrugged.

Adele squeezed her hand and then jumped down from the stool. "I'll leave you alone now, if that's okay. I think I might finally be tired enough to get some sleep."

"Didn't you just drink a whole cup of coffee?" Cassie asked.

"It's decaf," Adele said over her shoulder as she left the kitchen.

"Now you're the one who's going to get kicked out of the club!" Cassie called after her.

Cassie poured the useless beverage down the sink and sat in the quiet kitchen for another half hour. The scenes flashed in her mind again—the pale light reflecting off a stone wall and a woman lying on a table. Cassie clutched her head in her hands. Then she stood up, grabbed her coat and her keys, and headed straight for Eli's house.

17

"I am *not* going to do that," Eli said. "Cassie, listen, I'm sorry. I know that you're going through a lot. But this is not one of your fun adventures you can talk me into."

It had taken Eli a few minutes to wake up and realize that he wasn't imagining Cassie outside of his window, relentlessly tapping against the glass. Since it was 5 a.m., he guessed that it was a good thing she hadn't tried the front door.

"Eli, I've been thinking about it, and this could be our only way of finding more evidence. Whatever is going on in my head, it's connected to that manual. What if we can find something in my mind that proves that a member of the Roscoe family has been practicing memory murder?"

"It's too dangerous, Cass. There's a reason they have laws against this kind of thing. I don't have enough training."

"I know there's more in my head, but I can't reach it. Eli, you can do a session on your own. You already have the memory key—the cavern. I don't have to explain it to you since you've been there. It'll be easy to find. You've been apprenticed for months now. You're basically of age to practice."

"I have another two years until I can even try to go before the Council to obtain my full license."

"Ronan brightened a memory after a few weeks."

"He was doing it with a licensed luminator. If we get caught, I could get banished from Islayne. Hell—I could die, and you could go crazy."

"Before, you said you wouldn't be able to live with yourself if someone was doing this, and you didn't do anything to stop it. Well, this is your chance to do something. This might be the only way we figure out the truth!"

"Shhh! You're going to wake someone else up."

She put her hands on either side of her head. "I can't stand this," she said. "I have to know. I keep seeing this unconscious woman lying on a table in the cavern. I keep hearing that scream, and I don't know how much longer I can take this pain. I feel like I'm going crazy. Please. You're the only one who can help me."

She slouched against the edge of his window, looking like all the fight had gone out of her. Eli studied her face briefly. Even though she was clearly exhausted, with dark circles under her eyes and her normally perfect hair sticking up in all directions, she was so beautiful. And he could tell what a huge toll this was taking on her.

He took a deep breath, picturing the way she'd looked at him when he'd first opened the window—as if he was exactly what she needed. And she was right, Ronan did revive his first memory after only a few weeks...

"I'll do it," he said.

"Oh my God, really? Thank you!"

"On one condition."

"Anything."

"Afterwards, you have to go on a date with me."

RONAN AWOKE to the sound of someone incessantly ringing the doorbell. He stumbled down to the front door in a haze of sleepiness and opened it to find Adele frantically pacing back and forth on his front porch. Ronan was suddenly very aware of his bedhead, lack of deodorant, and wrinkled Star

Wars pajamas. He silently cursed his mum for the Christmas present. But he didn't have any more time to contemplate his appearance as Adele rushed inside.

"How did you get here?" he asked.

"I stole Cassie's bike. Please, you have to come help. I think she is about to do something really stupid."

"That's not news, Adele. Cassie does stupid stuff all of the time."

"No this is different—I think she's going to get Eli to revive her memories."

"What?! That's crazy!" Ronan exclaimed. "Why would you think that?"

Adele quickly filled Ronan in on her conversation with Cassandra much earlier that morning.

"I woke up pretty late this morning, and I realized she was gone," Adele said. "I thought maybe I was just being paranoid, but then I went to Eli's house, and their maid said he wasn't there, either. Ronan, I think he's going to do it. Or, I don't know when she talked to him, maybe he's already doing it."

Ronan tried to calm down and think about this rationally. He wanted to believe that Cassie would never be so stupid as to try to convince Eli to do something like this, but he didn't. When Cassie got an idea into her head, it was almost impossible to get her to change her mind. And even though Eli said he was going to stand up to her more, Ronan knew that if Cassie truly wanted to, she would be able to convince Eli to do what she asked. Dread pooled in Ronan's stomach.

"Let's go," he said to Adele, not bothering to change clothes. "If you're right, there's only one place in the district Eli would try this."

Twenty minutes later, Ronan and Adele arrived outside an old, condemned office building on the outskirts of the Lumin District. Ronan had only been here once before, last summer, when Cassie had the bright idea to try to climb to the top of the domed workroom. He thought that would be the most reckless thing she ever tried in this place. Ronan told Adele on the drive over that the building had been scheduled for demolition for months now, but there was some kind of hang up with the Council zoning ordinances, so nothing had happened yet. Even though it was falling apart, it would still have the sound-muffling design of the workroom that would keep the noise of the session in check.

Cassie's vehicle sat alone in the small car park. The boards that had been nailed to the front door of the office were torn off and lying in the dirt. Ronan cursed when he saw it and rushed inside, Adele close behind him.

If Ronan thought Ben's office was in bad shape when he'd first seen it, it was nothing compared to this place. The smell of mothballs assaulted him as soon as they walked inside. The furniture in the parlor was faded and full of holes, and Ronan heard the sound of rodents scampering away from their presence. They saw fresh footprints left in the thick layer of dust on the floor. Adele made as if to open the door to the workroom, but Ronan grabbed her hands to stop her.

"Wait. Before we go inside, I need you to promise me that you'll stay at least ten feet away from Eli and Cassie. That area right around them, the pullspace, could be really dangerous for you if he's started a session. Only the people inside that area are affected by the magnetism of the memories, so just stay along the back wall, and you'll be safe. Okay?"

She nodded. He held her hands for a beat longer than necessary, and then dropped them to open the workroom door.

As they stepped inside, Ronan's heart starting pounding. From the light of the mindscape stretched across the dome of the workroom, he could see Cassie lying in a long, reclined chair, her eyes closed. Eli was to the right of her, looking exhausted and drained as he pulled a cluster of memories closer. Ronan wondered how long he'd been in session; he motioned to Adele to keep quiet. The last thing he wanted was to break Eli's concentration when he already looked on the verge of collapse.

Even in his state of half-panic over his friends, Ronan couldn't help but notice that there was something wrong with the memories in the grouping Eli had selected. They were all centered around the cavern, and some of them—the ones Cassie had formed recently when they were exploring—looked healthy and normal, like most recent memories did in a client's mind. But there was one old one that looked ragged and tattered. The memory wasn't simply drained of color and energy like a normal older, fading memory. Instead it was shredded, like someone had taken a knife to it. The memory was barely still attached to others in the cluster.

Eli must have noticed it too because he pulled that particular memory forward, letting it grow large until it was about the same height as him. Maybe it was because the memory looked wrecked, or maybe because he was distracted by his curiosity, but whatever the reason, Eli must have let his control slip. Ronan saw Eli gasp as the pull of the memory descended down on him. He immediately fell to his knees from the force of it, and then he began to slide forward.

Ronan heard Adele make a noise, like a muffled scream, but it sounded as if it were coming from far away. Ronan was already running toward Eli. As soon as he crossed over into the pullspace, he felt the magnetism of the scene wrench the air from his lungs. He forced himself to slow down, driving his own concentration against the memory as he did so. It seemed to take ages, but he finally reached his friend, and then just as Ben had done multiple times for him, Ronan shoved Eli out of the pullspace, and then took his place in front of the memory. The only difference was that Ben had years of training and a massive amount of mental concentration to control memories while Ronan had only been doing this for a few weeks. He tried not to think about the consequences if he failed. Instead, he recalled everything his trainer had taught him. He focused and pushed back against the memory, trying to mentally shove the force back into the scene in front of him. After a few terrible seconds, he felt the pull slowly relent.

Good, now he could end this session and yell at his friends. He started to push the memory back into the cluster when the wrongness of it struck Ronan again. Though the practical, rule-following part of him was screaming for him to stop and end the session, Ronan couldn't help himself. He began to feel out the memory, finding where it was weak and drained of color, and letting the healing desire grow in him. Like before, he allowed the sense to develop and then eventually, pushed it into the scene in front of him. There were no bright lights or loud sounds. But he felt the memory revive slightly, and then quickly begin to fade again. Ronan did the same thing over. This time it brightened for longer, but then dulled once more. Ronan decided to try once more, waiting until the desire grew even stronger, and then pushed it into the memory. But this time, as soon as it brightened, Ronan let the entire memory play out in front of him.

The sound of waves lapping up against the shoreline flooded the workroom. It was mostly dark, but in the corner of Cassie's vision, Ronan could see moonlight spilling onto a small, leather bound book. Ronan recognized the strange markings on the cover. He heard the sound of a motor cut off, the clang of metal-on-metal, and then he saw a hand reach down and grasp the book. After a few moments of silence, Ronan heard cloth rustling, and then despite the rips in the scene, he could make out the beach and cave opening they'd explored a few weeks before. He realized that Cassie must have been hiding under a blanket or sheet in a boat. Looking through her eyes, Ronan could see a light emanating from the cave in front of her, growing steadily dimmer as the person from the boat walked further into the opening. Cassie quickly began to follow, staying far enough away from the light so she couldn't be seen or heard. As she walked, Ronan recognized the familiar dirt floor and stone archways. Finally, after the many twists and turns of the pathway, Cassie came to the mouth of the cavern. It looked much more menacing without the daylight streaming through, awakening the brilliant colors of the stone. She kept to the darkness of the outer wall of the cavern and hid behind one of the small boulders.

As her unaware companion turned on two standing lamps on either side of a long metal table, Ronan could see Alister Murdoch's face clearly in the light. Ronan sucked in his breath sharply, and it took all of his concentration not to break his mental hold on the scene. Alister's dark blue eyes and prominent cheekbones mirrored those of his daughter as he gazed down at the leather-bound book all too familiar to Ronan. After a few more minutes of preparation in almost total silence, Ronan heard footsteps coming from the passageway. Three men that Ronan didn't recognize walked into the cavern, carrying a fourth—unmoving—person among them.

They roughly threw the unconscious person onto the long table. It was a middle-aged woman, small boned, with short black hair.

Ronan couldn't quite pick up the heated conversation between Alister and the other men, but from the luminator's gestures, it looked like he was arguing for them to go wait in the passageway. He seemed to win the discussion since they all filed out of the cavern a moment later. Alister placed his fingers at the woman's temples. He paused, as if debating something internally. Ronan wished Cassie had moved closer so he could make out the expression on Alister's face. But then the luminator closed his eyes, and the memories began to funnel out into the air.

Soon the mindscape encompassed the wide expanse of the cavern. After another half hour of searching, Alister found the memory he'd been looking for. Like Ronan had seen many times by now, Alister drew the memory close and enlarged it until it stretched to the height of a man. Because of Cassie's distance from Alister, Ronan couldn't make out many details of the scene, only that it looked like a forest at night, since he could see the moon half-obscured by branches.

Alister closed his eyes and looked to be focusing on something deep within himself. He stretched out his hands, and small rips appeared in the memory, growing steadily larger the longer that Alister concentrated. The dark colors of the scene began to drip out of those tears and then dissipate into the air. A loud, piercing scream filled the cavern and, by extension, the workroom. Ronan heard Cassie gasp and he lost sight of Alister as she hid her face in her hands. Ronan could feel the scream reverberating painfully inside his own head. It sounded like a tortured animal. Everything inside him begged for the noise to stop. But it didn't. It went on and on and on until he felt like the sound might drive him to the point of insanity. At some point, Cassie looked up from her hands again to see Alister in the exact same position, though from his posture, it looked like the effort was taking a huge toll on him.

Finally, just as Alister appeared to be close to fainting from the exertion, the memory collapsed in on itself and then disappeared, leaving a fine mist that melted away into nothing seconds later, along with the scream. Silence filled the cavern, but it was not a comforting sort of silence. It felt ominous, rushing in to fill a void that should not exist. Alister leaned forward, putting his hands on his knees. The other memories grew brighter, larger, and more menacing as Alister's mental control waned. He didn't seem to notice as he gasped for breath and wiped the sweat from his face. The memories were much closer now, circling the luminator like predators. Still, Alister remained oblivious to his danger.

"Daddy! The memories—watch out!" Ronan heard the voice of a much younger Cassie shout as she leapt from her hiding spot.

Alister's head snapped up in surprise. He stared at his daughter, his mouth open in shock. Then, as if suddenly realizing what she had said, he pulled his gaze away from Cassie and focused on the expanding memories surrounding him. With a last burst of mental effort, Alister forced the scenes under his control, pushing them back into the mindscape, and finally resting his hands on the woman's temples and funneling the memories back into her mind. Then he ran over to his daughter.

"Cassie, how in the world did you get here?" he said, but then he heard noises from the passageway. For the first time, he looked truly frightened. "We'll talk about this later. For now, I need you to go back into hiding. Don't say a word. I'll come get you after I finish. Do you understand?" He gently pushed her down behind the boulder before she could answer and ran back over to the woman as the men walked back inside.

After a few more minutes of muffled conversation, the men took the woman, handed over a briefcase, and left. Alister opened it briefly—just long enough for Cassie to catch a glimpse of the neat stacks of money—and then shut it again. Alister came back over to his daughter, a look of pained determination on his face.

"Daddy, what were you doing?" she asked.

He stroked her hair lightly. "What I had to do, sweetheart."

"What was that screaming?"

"Here, do you want to come see where daddy does his work sometimes? Do you want to come sit on this table?" he asked.

"But you said I could never come into the room where you work," she said.

"This is a special occasion," he said as he led her back to the middle of the cavern.

"Are you mad at me?" she asked when she was lying down on the table and her father's back was to her.

"No, darling, I'm not mad at you," Alister said, turning back around. He placed a hand on either side of Cassie's head. The last thing Ronan saw was the face of Cassie's father with his eyes full of tears, and then darkness fell.

18

Ronan's mind was spinning, reeling, refusing to believe the scene. In a haze of disbelief, he touched his fingers to Cassie's temples, siphoned the memories back into her mind, and ended the session. He still wasn't ready to accept that it was possible for any luminator to destroy someone's memories, much less that Alister Murdoch would be the one to do it. He'd been holding out hope that there was a reasonable explanation for everything they'd discovered. He'd been holding his breath, waiting for the bad dream to end, waiting until he could resume his normal life where his profession existed untainted.

And now, he realized, there was no waking up.

Ronan glanced over at Eli, but he was staring at the space where Cassie's memory had been moments ago. Ronan had never seen such unadulterated rage on Eli's face before; his friend looked angry enough to kill someone. Adele walked up next to them silently, her face like a mask, her eyes never leaving Cassie. Her earlier anger and franticness were gone, but it was as if no other emotion had taken their place.

A few seconds later, Cassie opened her eyes, looking disoriented from the after-effects of the session. Normally, clients would drink a cup of Longwood tea to help them more quickly overcome the typical nausea and dizziness, but since any tea left in this office would be food for the rats, Cassie had to overcome the side effects on her own.

She looked surprised to see Ronan and Adele there. "So, I guess you all figured out what we were doing?" she asked, steadying herself as she slowly sat up.

"It's a good thing too," Ronan said. "Otherwise you'd have landed yourself on the front page of the *Islayne Times*. Not that you would know, since you'd be insane, and Eli would be dead." He meant to sound more upset, but Ronan was still too shocked to be mad at Cassie.

She glanced at Eli, mistaking the source of his anger.

"Oh God, Eli, I'm sorry. I truly thought we would be okay, that it wouldn't be that dangerous. It's just...I felt so desperate. I had to know."

"I'm not mad about that," Eli said, his face softening as he stepped closer to her. "We're fine. And you were right. It was important."

"But...wait...I still don't remember anything. Could you not find it?" she asked, looking around at them.

"I found it," Ronan said quietly.

"What is going on?" Cassie asked, a note of panic edging into her voice. "You would normally be yelling at me for doing something so reckless. What did you see in my head that's making you treat me like I'm breakable?"

"Cassie, this memory, it might take you a while to recall it, if you ever do. I don't know," Ronan said. "The memory was in bad shape—I'd never seen something like it before—and when I tried to brighten it, the effect wasn't lasting."

"But you let it play, right? So tell me about it!"

Ronan could see the helpless woman, laying unconscious on the table. He could hear the scream of the dying memory. He shuddered. He couldn't talk about it yet. He wasn't ready to relive what he'd witnessed.

"I don't think we should stay here any longer," Adele said.

"But I need to know—"

"What if someone catches us here, Cass?" Adele reasoned with her. "I think you guys could get in a lot of trouble."

"She's right," Ronan said, happy to have a reason to put off talking about

Cassie's memory. "Someone might have heard that scr- I mean, that session. It was louder than normal. We should go now."

"Okay fine," Cassie said. "My house is closest."

Eli and Ronan exchanged a glance over Cassie's head.

"Your dad's still gone?" Ronan asked.

"Yeah. Why?"

"It's nothing," Ronan said. "Let's just go."

They all piled into Cassie's car, with Eli in the driver's seat. Ronan tried to force himself to face what he'd just seen in Cassie's head. Alister Murdoch destroyed someone's memories for money. One of the most celebrated luminators on the island betrayed everything that their trade upheld in return for a briefcase full of cash. Those were the facts. Ronan's head ached.

For as far back as he could remember, Ronan loved lumination and revered those who practiced it. But as he got older, and especially after manifesting the gifting himself, he began to see the chinks in the armor—the greed and corruption of the old families, the bias of so many luminators against new blood, the difficulties of trying to make a living in the trade. But Alister Murdoch stood apart from all of that. Not only had Ronan respected him for all that he'd accomplished in the face of so much opposition, but he'd loved Alister for his mission to make a better and fairer world for luminators. Ronan believed in the vision Alister had been working so hard to cast for so many years. He was a symbol of hope to Ronan, and to countless others, that they had a shot at achieving something even without the old blood running through their veins. He made Ronan believe that his worth wasn't found in his heritage or where his parents were born.

Now, all of that felt hollow and tainted.

The minutes passed in silence until they pulled up in front of Cassie's house, filed out of the car, and sat sprawled out around her front porch.

"Okay, no more delays," she said once they sat down. "What happened?"

Ronan recounted the events of the past hour—from Eli nearly getting swallowed whole to the strange nature of the cavern memory to the details of the memory itself. Cassie listened silently the whole time.

"You're saying my dad did that to some helpless woman? And to me?"

she asked incredulously when he'd finished. "But, that's impossible. That would mean, he's a...he's a monster."

"Yeah," Eli blurted out angrily. "He is."

"But hold on," Adele said. "How do we know that the memory is real? It looked different than the other memories. Maybe it was just a weird dream, or a false memory or something."

Ronan shook his head. "Luminators only have control over real memories, not dreams. And a false memory doesn't actually exist. That's just your brain filling in portions of a faded, true memory. Everything that luminators can bring out of someone's mind—those scenes have all really happened."

Just then, Cassie cried out and cradled her head in her hands. Ronan realized that the memory was coming back to her. He motioned for Adele not to reach out to her, since he knew human touch would only make the strange sensation worse. They sat in pained silence, punctuated only by Cassie's occasional gasp or, near the end, soft crying. Finally, Cassie slowly raised her head. Her eyes were red, and she looked even paler than before.

"I remember it now," she said. "You're right. He did it. To her, and...to me."

"But he couldn't have," Adele said.

"Adele stop defending him! I'm telling you I remember it—" Cassie began.

"Exactly," Adele said gently. "You can recall it. How could you do that if he destroyed the memory? Maybe...he started to, but then he couldn't finish it. Maybe he just damaged it enough that you couldn't bring to mind until now."

"Oh, well, if that's all he did, I guess I don't have any reason to be upset!" Cassie spat.

"Of course you do," Eli said, his voice tight with anger. "What your dad did was unthinkable. I wanted to kill him when I saw that memory, Cass. So what if he didn't go through with it on you? He meant to. He started to, and he did go through with it on that woman and who knows how many others? He could still be doing it now. We need to stop this. We should go before the Council. We have to make sure this never happens again."

Ronan's head snapped up at Eli's words. He'd been so caught up in his own personal feelings about Alister's actions that he hadn't even thought about the larger consequences of what he'd done. If they reported this to the Council, if this came out to the general public, there was no doubt that the old families would use it to sway opinion in their favor. They would elevate Alister's disgrace as an example of the corruption of new luminators, and they would take every opportunity the news afforded to consolidate power even further into the hands of a select few. Alister wouldn't earn his seat on the Council. All of the reforms that he'd been fighting for would be lost.

Surprisingly, Ronan realized there was a big part of him that didn't care. Alister's actions made the whole trade feel polluted. For the first time in his life, Ronan wondered whether his ability was more curse than gifting. What right had he to meddle in anyone's mind? If Alister had never had the power to access someone else's memories, that poor unconscious woman from the cavern would still have a fully-intact past. The scream filled his mind again, and he shuddered. Before, he'd always thought of Islayne as special since it was the only place in the world where lumination existed. Now, he began to wonder if the water surrounding the island was a way to protect the rest of the world from his power and others like him. Maybe this gifting should never have existed in the first place.

He thought back to Jillian's memory he'd brightened just a few days ago. He remembered the feeling of awe and contentment as the life rushed back into the scene. It had felt so *right* to do that. But maybe it had felt right that night to Alister, too. Ronan hated that he shared the same gifting as that man. His mind flitted to the image of the memory ripped and bleeding, of the woman lying unconscious. Rage flooded through him.

"Wait, I'm not sure I'm ready for that," Cassie said to Eli. "I need some time. This is a lot to take in."

"What's to take in?" Eli asked. "What he did was evil."

"He's still my dad, Eli! I deserve a few days to think about bringing him up on criminal charges."

"I'm with Eli on this," Ronan said, feeling lightheaded and reckless. "Alister deserves justice."

"Maybe we should take some time, let Cassie process this, and then come up with a plan," Adele suggested.

"Here's a plan," Eli retorted. "Go to the Council and tell them we have evidence that Alister Murdoch has been destroying people's memories."

"I'm not ready to do that!" Cassie snapped at him.

"This isn't just about you Cass! Your dad could still be doing this. We have to protect people from him."

"If people like your parents hadn't made it so hard for my dad to find work in the first place, then maybe none of this would have happened!" Cassie shouted.

Her words might as well have been a slap. Eli stared at her. "So that's how it is? After all this time, after everything we've been through, my opinion doesn't matter because of who my parents are? That's funny—that sounds *exactly* like their philosophy."

Cassie looked like she wanted to say something in return, but then she closed her mouth and looked away, tears brimming in her eyes.

"You two need to go," Adele said firmly, leaving no room for argument. "Cassie you should go lie down. Let's talk about this tomorrow."

Ronan didn't want to talk more. He wanted to act. And from the look on Eli's face, Ronan thought he must feel the same. They both stood up. Ronan checked his phone. 12:00 p.m. He realized he was supposed to be at Ben's office in half an hour. Even though he felt angry and conflicted about lumination, he knew he couldn't just skip his apprenticeship without incurring Ben's wrath. But that didn't mean he couldn't do something about Alister right afterwards. As soon as they were safely out of earshot of the girls, Ronan turned to Eli.

"I have to be at my apprenticeship soon, but meet me there at six. We can go report Alister to the Council together."

CASSIE WATCHED LISTLESSLY as Eli and Ronan drove away. Her headache had finally dissipated, as if her mind could be quiet now that it had relayed the truth to her. Adele walked inside, came back out a few moments later with a steaming cup of tea, and placed it next to her. Cassie's arms felt too heavy to lift, and her throat felt too tight to swallow anything. but it was still a nice gesture.

Cassie looked out over the tall trees at the edge of her yard and let her thoughts wander aimlessly. She thought of the time that Adele and her mom, Gina, came to visit when both the girls were obsessed with the *Anastasia* soundtrack. They begged Gina to play *At the Beginning* every time they got in the car, and every time she said yes. She remembered when she and Adele dyed their hair bright pink without telling Gina first, but instead of getting upset when she found out, she asked them to dye her hair too. She remembered the three of them building an elaborate fort in her foyer out of all the sheets in the linen cupboard, and the thrill she felt at getting to spend the night in sleeping bags on the cool wood floor instead of in her bed. She remembered so many nights staying up late with Adele, whispering solemn secrets and sharing jokes that would only ever be funny at 3 a.m.

Adele laid her hand on Cassie's arm as she sat next to her, trying to silently comfort her. Adele and her mum were the same in that way—they never talked much when someone else was upset. They sat, touched, waited, completely at ease with the quiet. Cassie remembered Gina's cool hand cupping her cheek and wiping away her tears after her mother's funeral. She remembered Gina pulling her into her lap and stroking her hair, not saying a word. Silence had never felt so full of love.

She didn't have any memories of her father at the funeral, only Gina. Why hadn't her father been the one to hold her, to kiss her? All her life, Cassie had suppressed those kinds of questions. She'd always forgiven her dad for his busyness and long absences from her life. He had his reasons. First, it was because he was grieving, then it was because he was doing important work. She'd never begrudged him the missed bedtime stories or parent-teacher conferences. She used to imagine what it would be like to have a father who yelled at her for missed curfews or always remembered to pick her up from school. But her dad wasn't like that. And it was fine, it was fine, she'd always convinced herself, because he was Alister Murdoch. He was fighting the old families for fairness in the trade. He was the champion of the everyday luminator. He was a hero, *her* hero. And if his forehead kisses and breakfast conversations were few and far between because of everything he was working to accomplish, the rarity of those occasions made them all the more valuable.

Cassie saw her father with his hands raised, the memory with large gashes torn in it, the woman laying helplessly on the table. Her stomach tightened again. She would never make another excuse for Alister Murdoch ever again.

19

When Ronan arrived at Ben's office, no one was there. His trainer had probably left for lunch. In the silent room, Ronan replayed the images from Cassie's memory over and over in his mind, feeding his anger at Alister. And yet, in these familiar surroundings, other thoughts kept stubbornly popping up in his mind. He couldn't help but remember the rush he felt each time the mindscape poured forth from Jillian's head and filled the domed ceiling of the workroom. He recalled the awe he felt the first time he watched Ben at work—fully at peace, fully focused. Once again, the pure *goodness* of a brightened memory filled his senses. Was he ready to put the future of every new luminator in jeopardy just to make sure Alister paid for his actions?

Jillian walked into the parlor at that moment, interrupting his thoughts.

"Oh, Mrs. Poe," Ronan said, jumping up at the sight of her. "I don't think your session is supposed to start for another half hour."

"Really?" Jillian asked, looking down at her watch. "I'm so sorry. I must have gotten it mixed up in my calendar."

"Well, would you like to take a seat?" Ronan asked, half-hoping she would decline his offer and come back closer to her appointment time. "I just got here. I think Ben stepped out for a few minutes."

"I suppose this is as good a place to wait as any," Jillian said.

They sat in slightly uncomfortable silence for a moment. Ronan's mind began to wander back to the morning's events.

"You don't like me very much, do you?" Jillian asked suddenly.

The unexpectedness of the question jolted him out of his reverie. He wasn't sure how to answer her. In the past few weeks, he'd wondered from time to time why Jillian was having memories of Anthony revived instead of ones of her husband, but he'd mostly come to agree with Ben that it wasn't his place to know.

"I...haven't really thought about whether I like you, if you want the truth. I think about how we can do our best work for you."

She laughed lightly. "I appreciate your candor. But on that first day, you were surprised by my deception on the application, and you didn't approve. I could tell."

"It's really none of my business," Ronan began.

"Please," Jillian said, holding up her hands. "I would like to tell you why. I don't mind if people dislike me for true reasons, but if possible, I like to clear up the false ones."

Ronan almost tried to dissuade her again, but he stopped himself. There was no Council ruling that said he had to try to force a client not to share their reasons behind their sessions. And if nothing else, it might get his mind off of Alister for a while. He could use the respite.

"Okay," he said.

"I asked for these specific memories, not to disrespect my husband, but to put long-standing fears to rest. Anthony was a man I knew when I was still a child. Well, at your age, you might have considered me more of an adult, but looking back on it now, I know that I was not old enough to truly understand much about life. We fell in love the way only some young people can, the ones untouched by care or tragedy. It seemed effortless and easy and all-consuming. We got engaged when I was seventeen. And then, a few months before our wedding, Anthony died in an automobile accident.

"Three years later, I met Phillip. Two years after that, we were married. We had a full life together—four children, eleven grandchildren—and I loved him. He passed away last year. But, in all of that time, whenever we had an argument or we didn't have enough money or one of our children fell ill, I would be tormented by doubts. That somehow, if only Anthony hadn't died, my life would have been better, richer, fuller. That we wouldn't have had these difficulties or fights.

"After Phillip died, I decided I needed to truly understand what my time with Anthony had been like. I used most of our retirement money to come here to find out. But I didn't want my children to know, so I lied on my application in case they came across it."

"And what have you found?" Ronan asked.

She paused for a moment, as if gathering her thoughts. "My life with Phillip was real and beautiful," she said finally. "With the memories I have of Anthony now, I realize how little I truly knew him. Oh, our time together was fun and exciting and I did love him, but not in the same way I came to love Phillip—cemented in a lifetime of shared experiences, both good and bad ones. If Anthony hadn't died, then I believe we would have gone on to have a full life together, but it would have had its own difficulties. That head-over-heels, carefree love doesn't last. By giving me back those early memories, I can see my whole life more clearly now. Those doubts I struggled with for so long are finally quiet."

Something clicked in Ronan's mind as Jillian finished speaking. It was as if her revelation had roused him from the murk, reminding him of everything good about lumination, everything this trade could offer to the world. Lumination gave people a fuller life. The trade wasn't polluted just because of the actions of one man. He still hated what Alister had done, but he didn't hate his gifting. He could never hate this trade. More than anything, Ronan realized he still wanted to practice. He wanted to prove, in part to himself, that luminators could still use their power and use it well.

"Thank you for telling me," Ronan said, and he meant it.

"What do you mean you changed your mind?" Eli asked when Ronan met him in front of Ben's office a few hours later. Ever since his conversation with Jillian, Ronan had been trying to decide what he would say to Eli. He knew that Alister still deserved to be held accountable for what he'd done—

and maybe was still doing somewhere—but he also wasn't ready to jeopardize his whole future and the future of every other new luminator.

"What will happen to all of the reforms that Alister is championing if we turn him in right now?" Ronan asked. "We would lose all of our forward momentum. He won't get a Council seat. Nothing will change."

"Are you telling me that after what you just saw, you still *want* someone like him on our Council?" Eli asked.

"No, I'm not saying that. But maybe we can find a way to sort this out privately, without the whole world finding out what's happened."

"I think the world should find out about this," Eli said. "And if you won't talk about it, then I will."

If this comes to light, Ronan thought. *I could lose everything.* In many ways, Alister represented the new luminators. So his sins would become all of their sins. As much as Ronan hated what he'd done, that wasn't fair to everyone else. And it wasn't fair to him.

"Well that's easy for you to say!" Ronan said, his voice rising. "If everyone finds out what Alister's done, it won't totally ruin your career!"

Eli glared at him. "So you're joining in with Cassie now, huh? My opinion is a moot point because of my parents? I don't even want to be a part of this trade!"

That was the last thing Ronan had expected Eli to say.

"What are you talking about?" he asked. "You…you don't want to be a luminator? But then why are you doing it?"

Eli gave a short, harsh laugh. "My parents will put up with a certain amount of…mischief from me. But if I tried to choose another career path, that would be dishonoring the family name. They would disown me without a second thought. My parents might not be my favorite people in the world, but I'm not sure I'm ready to be without a family yet." He kicked the ground and looked miserable.

"Eli, I don't know what to say. I had no idea. I'm sorry."

"Yeah, well, now you know, and now maybe you can stop accusing me of only wanting to do this because my career is safe from the repercussions. I don't care about my career, but I do care about making Alister pay. Ronan, you saw what he did. He doesn't deserve to be protected."

"I don't want to protect him, but I want to be smart about this."

"So what would that mean, exactly? Because this isn't just about making sure he doesn't do it again. It should be about bringing him to justice for what he's done."

"Listen, Eli, I hate what I saw in Cassie's mind. It makes me sick. But if it comes to light, who knows what could happen? What if your parents and the others are able to close the profession to new luminators? I don't think one man's mistakes should be able to ruin it for everyone else."

"I think you're trying to justify keeping this a secret."

"You might not want to be in this trade, but this work means everything to me. And I finally have a shot at making a living as a luminator. If everyone finds out what Alister has done, I'll lose that chance."

"I get that. Really, I do. But this is bigger than just you," Eli said.

Ronan ran his hands through his hair in frustration. "Okay, can you just give me a few days to try to figure something out? Then I'll go with you to the Council. I promise."

Eli kicked at the ground again.

"Okay, two more days, but that's it."

A few minutes later, Ronan got in his car and headed home. In the silence, it was as if he could hear the clock ticking, counting down the precious little time he had to find a solution.

20

ALISTER MURDOCH LOOKED AT HIS SCHEDULE. FULLER THAN NORMAL, BUT that was to be expected after being gone for a few days. He'd probably have to push a few of his memory sessions to next week to make time to prepare for his interview with the *Islayne Times* later on today and then his meeting with his publicity team tomorrow. If he'd known how many sacrifices he would have to make to gain a seat on the Council, he might never have started trying four years ago. But it was too late for that now. Ever since his first campaign, he'd become a kind of celebrity on the island. Everyone loves an underdog, and every year, he'd gotten closer and closer to that majority vote.

This year, he thought it might actually happen. Then it was only a matter of time before he could start advocating for his new initiatives and start pushing back against the old families' influence on the Council. Bribery had always been illegal. He was going to make sure the law finally started to be enforced. Yes, change might truly be on the horizon. Alister hadn't been this excited about the future since he'd first manifested his gifting.

The sound of his study door slamming shut jarred him from his thoughts. He looked up to see Cassie, near to tears. He felt the familiar twin pulls of love and guilt that he always experienced when contemplating his daughter, ever since that night in the cavern eight years ago. There was a part of him that wanted to avoid her, but he never allowed himself that luxury for long. He would disappear into his work for a week or two, when the guilt became too much to bear, but he would always come back. Because he loved her, because that is what a good father would do, and because her presence was his penance. He would look at her, and then he could never fully forget the man he'd been. It made his life more difficult, but it also helped keep the demons at bay.

"Cassie, are you okay?" he asked, pouring more concern into his voice than he felt.

"You're back early," she said flatly.

"Yes, it didn't take as long as I thought it would to get Taylor's backing," he said. "He's very optimistic about my chances this year."

"Bully for you."

Secretly, Alister felt relieved. In the rare times that Cassie was in a bad mood around him, it was easier to justify his desire to get away from her. It felt like the kind of thing a loving father would do—create boundaries and maintain discipline. No one faulted a parent for sending a disrespectful teenager to her room.

"I'm not sure I like your tone," he began in his most serious fatherly voice.

"I'm not sure I give a shit."

Alister was taken aback by his daughter's words. Cassie might be moody occasionally, but she *never* spoke to him like that.

"Young lady, I don't know what has gotten into you today, but—"

"Don't worry Dad," Cassie cut him off, her tone falsely bright and furious. "If this conversation bothers you, I'm sure you can figure out a way to erase it from your mind. You sure seemed to get enough practice doing it on me."

Alister froze. For a moment, he wondered if he'd imagined the last words out of his daughter's mouth. Perhaps all of his exhaustion from traveling was catching up to him. For years after the fact, Alister wondered what it would be like if his daughter ever remembered that terrible, terrible night. He'd think about her confrontation with a kind of relief, as if he'd been dangling on the edge of a precipice for so long, and now finally, he could drop, no longer in limbo. But as the years went by, he began to worry about it—and hope for it—less and less. He worked out his own penance for his actions. Cassie didn't need to remember, because he bore the weight of every sight and sound from that night in his mind. The other times and other victims sometimes blurred together. But every blistering detail from that night was burned into his memory.

He wasn't prepared for this. How could she remember now? This wasn't supposed to happen. He searched his mind for the right words. Not the whole truth—that would forever be too painful. But a partial one. Like a tonic mixed with enough sugar to make it bearable to drink.

"Cassie, I never meant to hurt you."

She laughed. It was a new sort of laugh—bitter and hard—that Alister had never heard from her before. "That's the best you can come up with, Dad? That stupid, cliché line that's been in a thousand films and books? I don't care what you *meant* to do. I care about what you did. You make me sick. I can't believe I looked up to you, trusted you." Her voice broke for a minute. "You wanted to go into my mind, destroy *my* memories?"

"I was trying to protect you," he said. "I know, better than anyone, what witnessing that can do to someone. I didn't want you to have to live with that image, that noise." Even as he said it, the memories came flooding back. Those dark nights in the cave. The long queue of unconscious people, night after night. It *was* terrible, and yet...

"You know how you could have protected me, Dad? By not being the kind of monster who would do that in the first place. What about that woman? How exactly were you trying to protect her?"

"You don't understand," Alister said. "I didn't have a choice. I was about to lose my luminator license. I couldn't clock enough hours and pay the fees and work my second job and take care of you. I was going lose everything I'd fought so hard for. I didn't do it for long, just a year. Just enough to pay the bills and keep my license. Once we were in the black, I stopped. I haven't done it in a long time."

Yes, that was the way to spin it. Only talk about the desperation. Only talk about the money.

"Oh, well as long as you didn't want to do it," Cassie said, biting off each word. "As long as you didn't do it for long, then what am I upset about? Now it all makes sense."

"You're still young, Cassie, and you've never had to worry about money. You don't understand the kind of pressure I faced."

"Don't patronize me. Don't act as if I don't have a right to hate you. Does it bother you at all that everyone thinks you're this role model for luminators when really, you went against everything that your profession stands for? How can you try to land a Council seat after doing what you've done?"

"I'm trying to do that so that no other luminator is ever forced to make the kind of choices that I had to make. It's fine if you want to blame me, but you should also blame the Lydons, and the Roscoes, and those Brenningtons you're so fond of. If it wasn't for their arrogance and corruption and greed, I would never have been forced to do something so terrible to make ends meet. I'm trying to make amends for what I did by taking away some of their power, so they can't control the trade and who practices it. That Council seat is my absolution."

She shook her head in disbelief. "It looks like you have it all sorted out. Well, I hope you memorized that speech, Dad. I'm sure your PR people will need all the help they can get to try and salvage your campaign once this comes to light."

Alister sighed. "Cassie, I know that you're angry at me, but coming forward with this won't do any good. You should know the Council law. After this many years, you can't submit your memory for evidence on its own. It would have to be combined with something tangible to cause reasonable doubt. And no one believes it's even possible to destroy memories."

"Not yet, but they'll probably be more likely to when I show them the book, and the cavern—with that very particular hum—where everything happened."

Time slowed down. Alister stared at his daughter. In all his old imaginings of what would happen if she recalled that night, it never came to this.

"You didn't just remember, did you?" he asked.

"No, I didn't," Cassie said, getting up and walking back toward the study doors. "You must be better at your work than you thought. But I found that cave with Ronan and Eli and Adele. We happened to find some other interesting artifacts there too. Eli and Ronan were hell-bent on exposing you once we figured out what happened. I tried to convince them to wait. Now, I'm not so sure they were wrong." She walked out the door.

Alister sat silently at his desk for a few minutes, willing his thoughts into order, willing the panic rising in his chest to subside. He remembered stumbling in the cavern on that last night, the book slipping from his grasp and falling into that deep hole. He knew he shouldn't have even brought it with him to the cavern sessions, but it was a comfort to have it close during those long nights. And on any other night, he wouldn't have lost his balance. But trying to do two sessions back-to-back, first with that woman and then with Cassie, he'd been nearly blinded by exhaustion at the end. He'd thought about going back with equipment, climbing down into the darkness, finding the book, and burning it. But it would have been too dangerous to do it on his own, and he couldn't have relied on anyone else to come with him. So he left it alone, trusting the darkness to hide his secrets. Now he was reaping the consequences of his carelessness.

He massaged his temples with his fingers, trying to calm down. He couldn't let Cassie go through with her threat. She didn't understand everything at stake here. His future was the final way to make up for his past. He could do so much good on the Council. He could make sure that all new luminators got a fair shot at the trade. Whatever he'd done in moments of desperation was nothing compared to what those families had done over years of calculated corruption. He could not allow anything to get in the way of the good he was so close to accomplishing.

He bent down and opened the bottom drawer of his desk. After tossing its contents, mostly old pens and loose sheets of paper, onto the floor, he pressed against the small latch at the back of the drawer. With a click, the bottom wood panel popped out, and he removed it to reveal another shallow compartment below. He traced the handgun lovingly, and the feel of the cool metal against his skin quieted his mind. He used to always carry this with him on those long nights in the cavern, never fully trusting his clients or the men they hired to carry out their wishes. The reassuring weight of it against his hip always helped to calm him before a session. Just the sight of the weapon brought back a host of memories.

He slammed the drawer shut. No, he couldn't. Not again. He'd promised himself he would never do it again. There was another reason for what he'd done all of those years ago, one that he could never tell Cassie, one that he only rarely admitted to himself. Yes, he had been desperate. Yes, he had needed the money badly. Yes, he couldn't bear the thought of giving up his work. But that wasn't the whole story.

The *other* feelings from those nights in the cave, the ones he always suppressed, came crashing down on him in an instant, like a wave that had been building for years, waiting for the right moment to break upon the sand.

He never knew how deeply grief could reach into a person's soul until Elise died. It was the suddenness of his wife's death that made it feel so unbearable. Maybe, if he'd had time to prepare, the torment of her departure wouldn't have been enough to fracture his whole being. But he'd had no time. One moment, she was there, and the next, she was gone. He was helpless in the wake of losing her. And it made all his memories of her feel sharp and cruel. He wanted to control something, anything, since he'd had no control over her death.

And so what he'd told Cassie was true—he was driven to his acts by a very practical desperation. After his wife's death, he had to find a way to care for their daughter alone, keep up his license, and pay the bills. But when he started tearing into that first memory, he felt such a catharsis. Finally, something he could dominate. It was a way to get back at all the memories that plagued him in his grief.

In some of the farthest recesses of his being, he *loved* that dark work in the cavern. There was a fragment of himself that relished the rush of power and the knowledge of his superiority. He didn't just have the ability to bend memories to his will, he could break them completely. That year had been both terrible and exhilarating—to see the rips appear in the scene, to watch as the memory's lifeblood dripped slowly away, dissipating to nothingness. He alone wielded such might over the almost-untamable memories. He'd felt so powerless in the hospital room, at Elise's funeral, at the door to

Cassie's room, hearing his daughter cry for her mother. But in the dark of the cavern, finally, he brandished power again.

Then afterwards, guilt and shame would wash over him as he watched the helpless, unconscious victim carted away. Every night, he would leave the cavern overwhelmed by remorse and yet, he could never quite silence the small part of him that savored the experience.

Until the night Cassie followed him. He remembered how she looked at him right before he forced her into the dream state. He remembered how it felt to touch her small head and will her memories to fill the cavern. As he found the most recent scene and started to rip it apart, that familiar, intoxicating sense of power rushed through him. Then he glanced down at his daughter, he saw how small and helpless she looked on the long table, and something broke inside of him. He saw himself for who he truly was, and he couldn't stand it. After ending the session, he vowed that he would never use his new abilities again. He vowed that he would be a dutiful father, and that he would work to make the trade easier for new luminators.

But now, he had to choose what portion of that promise to keep. His hand hovered by the drawer. *I'm doing this because I have to,* he thought. *I'm doing this for the good of everyone. I'm not doing this for me. I don't want this. I have to do this. I have to.*

He opened the drawer and picked up the gun. As he did, a small flicker of excitement passed through him. It had been too long.

21

Ronan pulled the memory closer to him. This one was more vibrant than most of the ones in the cluster, but it was still in need of some work. He tried to focus all of his concentration on the scene in front of him, but his mind felt sluggish and uncooperative. He'd barely slept the night before; he kept turning the day's discoveries over and over in his mind. He kept trying to figure out some way to make Alister pay for his wrongs while still protecting the rest of the luminator trade, but so far, he'd found no solution.

And he was running out of time.

As the memory grew steadily larger, Ronan thought back to the last time he brightened a scene—the tattered remains of Alister's work in his daughter's mind. For what must have been the hundredth time since yesterday, he saw the unconscious woman lying on the table, and he heard the terrible scream of the dying memory. He didn't know if he would ever get them out of his head.

"Ronan! What are you doing?!" Ben's voice brought him back to the present, and he realized a dozen memories were growing larger and beginning to circle him. He panicked and looked back at his trainer. Ben strode up next to him, taking control of the memories, and pushing them back into place. He turned on Ronan, his eyes blazing with anger.

"I, I'm sorry, I didn't think—" Ronan began.

"Leave this room and wait for me in my office," Ben cut him off, his voice low and furious.

The air felt stale in Ben's cramped office, as if the air conditioning couldn't be bothered to circulate to such a small, forgotten place. Ronan sat in the chair opposite his trainer's desk, fighting the insistent urge to break something. This was just perfect. Now on top of everything else going on, Ben was angry with him, too. Even in the stagnant heat of the room, Ronan shuddered as he thought of Jillian's memories beginning to circle him, making him feel like prey. Ronan could hear Ben talking to Jillian out in the parlor. They must have finished the session. Ronan knew he only had a few more minutes until Ben ushered Jillian out the door. He tried to ready himself for his trainer's anger. Just then, Ronan's mobile phone beeped loudly, notifying him of a text. He looked at the front of his screen to see a message from Cassie.

Please come to my house as soon as you can. I have to talk to you. Now.

As he was about to open his phone and reply, Ben burst through the door, startling Ronan and causing him to drop his phone. He could feel the anger coming off his trainer in waves as he took a seat across from him. Ronan didn't dare pick his phone up off the floor.

"Why are you here, Ronan?" Ben asked in a tightly controlled voice.

Ronan almost said, *Because you told me to wait in here*, but then he realized what the man was truly asking him. "I want to be a luminator," he answered, having a hard time meeting Ben's gaze. Ronan had never seen his trainer so mad.

"Do you? From the way you've been acting the past few days, I wouldn't know that. From what I just saw—I would think this trade is a joke to you."

Ronan opened his mouth to answer him, but Ben held up his hand to stop him.

"You were in *my* workroom," he continued, his voice rising. "With *my* client, you had her mind at your mercy—and you were *distracted*. What could possibly be so important to you that it would interfere in that moment? It is one thing to make a mistake while you are focused and trying, it is one thing to simply not have grasped a concept fully enough to execute

THE SECRETS OF ISLAYNE

it properly, but I will *not* tolerate you placing my client in danger because you have other things on your mind!"

"I'm sorry, please, I'm sorry," Ronan said. "I was exhausted, I couldn't sleep last night. You're right. I was distracted. But it won't happen again."

There was another beat of tense silence while Ben considered him. "When you began training with me, I found you, surprisingly, to be a promising student. In the first several weeks of your apprenticeship, you were focused, interested, hungry to learn. I made you work less because I was worried that you were *too* wrapped up in this trade, and that the lack of balance would lead to mistakes. But now I'm beginning to think we have the opposite problem. This past week, it's almost as if you aren't even here. You come in exhausted and distracted, you make thoughtless errors, and—worst of all—you don't seem to *care*. I am not in the habit of wasting my time. I need to know whether this is even a priority to you any longer. Because if it's not, I don't really see the point in continuing."

Ronan felt the panic rising in his chest at Ben's words. He knew he hadn't been as focused as he should have in his apprenticeship with everything else going on, and he'd had his doubts the day before, but he'd never voiced anything to his trainer, and he never thought his actions would be enough for Ben to question Ronan's drive to become a luminator. This was not how he'd envisioned this summer turning out. After that first session weeks earlier, when Ronan had realized that Ben was still incredible at this work and willing to teach him, Ronan had promised himself that he would take full advantage of what could be his one shot at this future. He was *not* supposed to have a conversation like this one, where Ben doubted his commitment to lumination, and his whole career might just hinge on convincing his trainer otherwise. Ronan's head began to pound at the thought of another thing now jeopardizing his future in the trade.

"I do want to be here! I'm not wasting your time. This past week has just been…insane. Everything that's happened. But I promise I will be focused from now on. Just please, don't stop training me. This is the only thing I want to do."

"Part of the discipline of being a luminator is the ability to shut out everything else that's going on, anything at all that could detract from your concentration, and to focus wholly on your client. If you can't learn to do that, then you'll be a danger to everyone."

"I *can* learn that, I know that I can," Ronan said, pleading. "Please give me the chance to show you."

Ben let out a long breath. "Okay then, tell me what happened this week."

"What?" Ronan asked.

"You said the problem was with everything that happened this week. I need to decide whether or not what happened was significant enough to warrant your carelessness in that session."

Ronan didn't know what to say. For a moment, he considered telling Ben everything—about the book, about the party, about what Ronan had once suspected of the Roscoes, about the illegal memory session, and about Alister's misdeeds. In a way, it would feel like such a relief to have someone else decide what to do. But what if he couldn't live with Ben's decision? It wasn't a risk he was willing to take.

"It's...personal," Ronan said.

Ben raised his eyebrows. "I tell you that your whole future might hang in the balance of the contents of this past week, and you only tell me it's personal? You see why I'm questioning your priorities?"

The weight of the past twenty-four hours seemed to suddenly drag Ronan down. He was tired of wrestling, tired of railing against Alister in his mind, tired of seeing no way out. He started yelling, not even fully aware of what he was saying, just to lash out at someone tangible instead of the ghost of the man he'd once respected.

"I can't tell you, and you don't have any right to ask me! And if you want to use that to screw me over, then fine. But I can't tell you because I have no idea what you'll do with the information, and this isn't just about me. You aren't the only person who has my future in their hands. I can't tell you because...it's too terrible, and I can still hear the screaming, and I can't get those images out of my mind! And no one should use their power like that, it shouldn't even be possible, but he did, and now, and now...and who the hell writes stuff down in Classical Gaelic anyways?!"

Ronan stopped suddenly, coming back to himself. *Oh God,* he thought.

Why am I yelling at him? Am I trying to make him dislike me even more? I need to get control of myself. I need some air.

"What did you say?" Ben asked, his eyes alight with something Ronan couldn't decipher.

"I'm sorry, I'm sorry," Ronan said, walking to the door. "I shouldn't have yelled. I just need a short break. I'll be back soon, please, don't stop training me. I'll explain everything when I get back."

"Wait, Ronan—"

But he'd already walked out the door, and he couldn't hear the rest of what Ben said. He couldn't afford to stay in that office. He was too worried that he would end up telling Ben everything, and he could not do that. He would take a walk, clear his head, and come up with a plausible lie to tell Ben when he returned.

Ronan reached down to pull out his phone before realizing that he'd left it in Ben's office. Then he remembered Cassie's text message. Ronan stood by his car and debated whether he should go. Maybe Ben was right, maybe his apprenticeship wasn't that important to him if he was willing to take more time to go meet Cassie instead of keeping to a short break like he promised. But then he remembered how small and frail his friend had looked after he told her about her memory. He couldn't abandon her while she was trying to process something this intense. He jumped in the driver's seat of his car and headed toward Cassie's house.

Ten minutes later, he knocked on her front door. But it wasn't Cassie who answered; it was her father. Before Ronan could react, Alister grabbed him by the front of his shirt, dragged him inside, and kicked the door shut. Ronan tried to fight back, but Alister shoved him hard, knocking him backwards onto the floor. Ronan scrambled up to his feet again to see Alister pointing a gun at him.

"Wonderful," Alister said. "You're the last guest to arrive. If you'd be so kind as to follow me."

22

BEN STOOD IN HIS OFFICE, DEBATING WHETHER HE SHOULD CHASE HIS apprentice down the street and demand an explanation for what had just come out of his mouth. He almost wondered whether the words had been a figment of his imagination. After so many years of searching for any clue as to the whereabouts of that book, he wouldn't put it past his brain to start creating hints out of thin air.

He opened and closed his fists. Then he heard Ronan start his car and drive away. It was too late to go after him now. He settled back into his chair. If Ronan knew something, Ben would get it out of him soon enough. The kid said he would be back soon, and besides, it was probably just a coincidence. What he said probably had no bearing on Ben's long, fruitless search at all.

Or are you just hoping that's the case? a skeptical voice sounded in his head. *Wouldn't it be easier if the past just stayed in the past?* He tried to ignore the doubts. Half an hour passed, and when Ronan didn't return, Ben started to get restless. He began to walk toward the door to the office when something caught his eye on the floor by Ronan's chair. It was his phone.

Ben knew he had no right to violate Ronan's privacy, but he had a sinking feeling that something was wrong here. He recalled how out of sorts and strange Ronan had been over the past week, and even though he was only a few minutes late, he'd never been late at all before. If anything, he always cut his breaks short.

Before he could talk himself out of it, Ben picked up the phone, breathed a sigh of relief that it wasn't password protected, and saw the latest text message from Cassie Murdoch. He'd forgotten that Alister had a daughter. Again he debated what to do. Her text sounded a little desperate, but it didn't mean anything was really wrong. A few more minutes passed, and when Ronan still hadn't returned, Ben began to truly worry. He decided to drive over to the Murdoch's home to see what was happening. Most likely, nothing was wrong, but he decided he'd rather be paranoid if everything was fine than deal with the guilt if everything wasn't.

23

Alister roughly tied Ronan's hands behind his back, threatening to use his gun if Ronan resisted. Then he hauled him up the stairs and down a hallway, to a corner room that Ronan had never been in before. Alister opened the door, pushed him inside, slammed the door shut, and locked it behind him.

"Ronan!" he heard Cassie shout, and he spun around to see Cassie, Eli, and Adele all similarly tied up. They were in a mostly empty room, with a few cardboard boxes stacked against one side and some mismatched pieces of furniture placed in a corner. The sunlight streamed in through a small window on the far wall, illuminating the dust particles dancing in the air.

"What happened?" he asked, still dazed.

"I confronted my dad," Cassie said in a small voice. "I told him what we knew. I told him I was going to expose him. I was so angry and hurt, and I needed to hear him admit to what he'd done. It was so stupid. But I never thought he would do something like this." She gave a harsh laugh. "Of course, I never thought he would be capable of destroying someone's memories, either. He got me and Adele first, and then Eli said he got a text message from me telling him to come to my house. I...I don't know what my dad is planning," she continued, a note of panic rising in her voice. "It's like I don't even know him at all. I am so sorry that I got you guys involved in this."

"Hey, you didn't get us involved in anything," Eli said. "If anyone's to blame, it's me. I was the one who translated the book. Wait, shit, where is it?"

"You brought it with you?" Ronan asked.

"Yeah because Cassie—or I guess her dad—asked me to. He must have grabbed it from me after he knocked me out."

"Eli," Cassie said. "I'm sorry about what I said before. I was still reeling from that memory session. I didn't mean it. I don't blame you—or your parents—for what's happened. My dad is responsible for his own actions."

As Ronan looked around at his friends, he tried to force down a rising sense of dread. It was his fault that they were here, helpless, at the mercy of a criminal. If he hadn't convinced Eli to wait to go to the Council, none of this would be happening right now. Things suddenly crystalized in his mind—there was no way to protect the new luminators and bring Alister to justice. He hadn't been willing to face that reality. Or perhaps, he wasn't sure until now which option he would choose.

He kept working at the ropes around his hands. The skin at his wrists began to chafe, but he ignored the discomfort. He thought he felt the ropes loosen just slightly.

"I should have listened to you in the first place," Ronan told Eli. "We should have taken what we'd found to the Council, and let them bring Alister up on charges. If we had, then we wouldn't be here now."

"But, you guys both wanted to do that," Adele began.

"But then I changed my mind," Ronan said, "Long story."

"Wow! An apology and an acknowledgement that I'm right," Eli said, a smile playing at the corners of his mouth. "You guys must really think we're not going to make it."

"Can you please not joke about that?" Adele said sharply. "We need to think of a way out of this. If we could find something to start cutting these ropes—"

But just then, the door swung open, and Alister's massive frame filled up the doorway. Before, Ronan had always found the man's size to be inspiring

—just another way that Alister Murdoch seemed larger than life. Now, for the first time, it was menacing.

"So sorry to keep you waiting," he said brightly, as if he was hosting a dinner party. Ronan noticed that his eyes looked bloodshot, as if he hadn't slept in a while. His normally smooth hair was tangled in knots at his shoulders, and his clothes were rumpled. The overall unkempt look unnerved Ronan. If Alister no longer felt the need to keep up appearances with them, was that because soon they wouldn't remember his appearance in the first place?

"Why are we here?" Eli asked, his voice threaded with tightly-controlled anger.

"For the good of the trade," Alister said.

"My parents will start to get suspicious if—" Eli began.

"Oh please, don't insult my intelligence by lying to me," Alister said gently, as if lovingly correcting a child. "Cassie has told me many times that your parents don't keep very close tabs on you, Eli. I'd wager they won't start to miss you for at least another day or two. I also know that Ronan's parents are on holiday, and Adele's parents are, of course, on the mainland. No, I happen to know for a fact that none of your families will notice your absence for quite some time. Long before it will ever be an issue. You needn't worry—I expect to have you all safely home within the next day."

Alister made his way over to Ronan, sparing a glance at Cassie. She refused to meet her father's gaze. For the briefest moment, Ronan thought he saw sadness pass over Alister's face, but then it was gone, replaced again by the false cheeriness. Alister looked at Ronan. "Come on, you first," he said. When Ronan didn't move, Alister sighed. "I would rather not knock you unconscious, but I will do so if you don't cooperate."

Ronan stood up. Alister pulled out the gun again, and beckoned Ronan to get in front of him. A moment later, Ronan felt the barrel of the gun pushed into his back. He didn't dare try to keep loosening the rope around his hands with Alister right behind him. "Walk slowly toward the door, please," Alister said.

"Where are you taking him?" Adele asked, her voice rising.

"Don't be frightened, Addy," Alister said softly, and Ronan saw Adele wince at the familiar nickname. "I'll be back soon." Ronan couldn't be sure if he meant it as a reassurance or a threat. He heard Alister lock the bedroom door behind them.

Alister led Ronan through the house, out into the backyard, and down through the familiar rocky path that cut into the cliff until they finally reached the Murdoch's private dock. A tiny motor boat, just big enough for two people, awaited them in the water. Alister pushed him into one of the seats, and then took more rope out of one of the boat's compartments and looped it through the chair and around Ronan's feet, securing him tightly. As soon as Alister couldn't see his hands, Ronan began working on loosening his ties again.

As Alister started the motor and steered the boat out into open water, Ronan thought back to all the times he imagined being Alister's apprentice. Even though the man had stopped taking on apprentices soon after Ronan started at the Academy, that never stopped Ronan from dreaming about what it would be like to train under him. All of those thoughts felt incredibly foolish now.

In far too short a time, the familiar break in the rocks came into view. Alister steered the boat toward the shallow beach in front of the cave, slowing them down until the boat coasted lightly onto the shore. *No,* Ronan thought as he tried and failed to pull his hands free. *I need more time.*

"Why are we here?" Ronan asked, hoping that Alister was in a chatty mood. Ronan stared up at the entrance that he and his friends had walked through only weeks before, though it now felt like a lifetime ago. Alister cut the motor completely and came back to where Ronan was seated. With a rising sense of dread, Ronan noticed that Alister was holding the leather manual in one hand.

The man looked at Ronan gently, as if he were trying to comfort him. "Come now, Ronan. You were always the brightest of my daughter's friends. Surely you've figured it out by now." His calmness unsettled Ronan more than if he were angry. Alister seemed completely at peace with the situation, which made Ronan think there would be no reasoning with him, no talking him out of what he planned to do.

"You're going to erase my memories," Ronan said flatly.

Alister nodded and gave him a small smile. "Don't worry. I know the prospect is frightening to you now, but soon you won't recall any of this. I will only destroy the memories that are absolutely necessary. I won't touch anything else in your mind. You have my word."

Even though Ronan had suspected that this was Alister's plan, the man's acknowledgment made it worse. It didn't make logical sense, but Ronan realized he'd been holding out hope that somehow, even at this point, Alister would redeem himself. Or at least, that he would show remorse over what he'd done and take responsibility for his actions. But now, Ronan knew that there would be no turning back.

"Your word isn't worth shit," he spat.

Alister nodded slowly. "I'm sure it must seem that way to you. But one day, you might understand that life forces us down paths we wouldn't normally choose. If I don't take care of this today, what you know could ruin the future of lumination for so many. People just like you, Ronan. I know that you're upset about what happened to Cassie, about some of the decisions I was forced to make in the past, but I can't let your misguided sense of justice wreck everything that I'm trying to accomplish. You can't see it, but I'm not being selfish. I'm doing what's best for the most people."

"Yeah? Was it best for your victims when you decided to rip apart their pasts?"

Alister's eyes hardened for a moment. "I had to provide for Cassie, so I made a difficult choice. As parents often do."

"I guess every assassin and drug dealer and pimp has a free pass as long as they're doing their jobs to make a living. You could have done a million other things to make money. You didn't have to do *that*."

"I did, actually. If I wanted to stay a luminator. I spent every day working to try to attract enough clients to clock enough hours, and at night, I did what I had to do so I could pay the Council fees and put food on the table. You should know these rules—they are the same ones that you will soon have to follow."

"Plenty of other luminators have made a name for themselves in this trade without stooping to do something so disgusting, so against everything we stand for. And if you couldn't manage it, then you should have just walked away."

Alister gave him a knowing smile. "Really? Do you think you could?"

"Yes," Ronan said, not deigning to show this man any evidence of his internal struggle. *Could I ever walk away from this?*

"Once I get a seat on the Council, you'll never have to back up that answer with actions. I'm going to guarantee that no other luminator has to make the kind of choice that I did. That's why we're here, Ronan, to make sure nothing stands in the way of progress. The kind of progress only I can bring about."

"Great—now I can add megalomaniac to cruel and self-deceived," Ronan muttered. There was a small part of him that knew it wasn't a good idea to antagonize the man who was armed and had him tied up, but Ronan was past caring.

Alister just shook his head, leaning in toward Ronan. "I won't expect you to understand, but I did what I had to do then, and I will do what I have to do now. It is a terrible thing, to have this kind of power. The ability to break something as wild and potent as a memory, that's something no one else in the world can understand. But I will wield my skills one more time, and then this will all be over."

Though Alister still seemed relaxed and in control, Ronan saw something flicker in his eyes as he spoke—it was hunger. The same kind of hunger Ronan felt when he thought about using his ability to brighten memories. With a start, he realized that Alister wasn't just doing this out of necessity, he was doing it because he *wanted* to.

Ronan tugged against his restraints again. Though loosened, the rope was still barely too tight against his wrists for him to pull free. But Ronan couldn't keep himself from acting. He jerked his head down sharply, slamming his forehead into Alister's face. He wasn't sure what he was expecting to happen, other than hoping to hit the man in exactly the right spot that he would be knocked unconscious. Instead, Alister yelled out in pain and reeled backwards, holding his nose. Then he brought the butt of his gun hard against the side of Ronan's skull. Even though it hadn't really helped anything, and even though the whole left side of his head now throbbed with pain, Ronan felt the tiniest bit better.

"Enough," Alister said gruffly. He carefully untied the cords around Ronan's legs, threw the rope over one shoulder, and then motioned for Ronan to climb out in front of him, making sure that he noticed the gun pointed firmly in his direction. Ronan made his way into the cave with Alister trailing behind him. They walked through the twists and turns of the passageway in silence, Ronan trying to sort out an escape plan in his mind the whole time. Eventually, they reached the familiar cavern, though this time, there was a long metal table situated in the middle of the stone floor.

As they neared the table, Ronan could feel that his restraints had finally loosened. He pretended to stumble and fell to one knee. As he heard Alister move closer to him, Ronan pulled one hand free of his restraints, turned, and brought the other hand across his body, whipping Alister in the face with the rope. The man recoiled back from the blow in surprise and dropped the gun. Ronan managed to grab the weapon off the cavern floor and scrambled to his feet before Alister could recover himself.

"Don't move," Ronan said, aiming the barrel of the gun squarely at Alister's chest.

Alister looked furious for a moment, but then quickly regained his calm. "Ronan," he said, taking a step closer to him. "Do you even know how to use one of those?"

"Do you really want to take that chance?" Ronan asked, pulling the hammer back. Silently, he thanked his uncle for that miserably hot day five years ago when he took Ronan shooting when he and his parents were visiting the mainland. Ronan had found it incredibly boring at the time, but now he could have kissed his uncle.

"You don't want to hurt me, Ronan," Alister said.

"Don't talk like you know me. I've seen firsthand what you're capable of. Cassie's memory made me sick."

"Firsthand?" Alister asked, and then Ronan could see the understanding dawn on him. "Of course, coming to the cavern didn't bring that memory back. You revived it, didn't you? My daughter has always had a reckless streak in her. She convinced you to do a session."

Ronan cursed under his breath. He hadn't meant to let Alister find that out. But ultimately, it didn't matter. No one would believe Alister once they found out about his past.

An annoying, shrewd smile spread across Alister's face. "You know it is in both of our best interests for me to follow through with this, Ronan."

"What, so you can make the luminator trade better for everyone? No thanks—I'll take my chances without you."

"That's not all," Alister said. "Have you considered what else will happen if Cassie comes forward with her memory?"

"What are you talking about?" Ronan asked, his curiosity piqued in spite of himself.

"You may not be familiar with how the Council deals with memories when presented as evidence. Let me enlighten you. Before the Council will accept any memory in a court proceeding, they will conscript a luminator to examine the mind of that individual and the memory in question. When Cassie's mind is examined, they will be able to tell that the memory was brightened. When no licensed luminator has a record of a session with her, my trial will still proceed, but they will also launch a separate inquiry to discover who practiced lumination without a license, and the first memories they will examine in that inquiry will be yours and Eli's. What will that examination turn up, I wonder?

"Now, I'm sure Eli was involved, but with his blood, I doubt he'll get more than a slap on the wrist. You, on the other hand, did revive her memory. That is most impressive, but I doubt the Council will share my opinion. They have a very strict punishment for practicing underage without a license. Banishment from Islayne."

Ronan just stared at Alister, the gun frozen in his outstretched hands, waves of dread hitting him. Everything Alister said made sense. How had Ronan not thought of this before? He knew that the Council required a luminator to verify a memory before it could be used as evidence, and he knew that a trained luminator could tell if a memory had been revived, but he'd never connected the dots. He'd just assumed that since no one discovered them during the illegal session, Ronan was safe, and no one would ever know. But of course, it would come out in the trial. Of course, there would be no record of an authorized session. Of course, that would lead to more questions. The questions would lead to an examination, which would lead to him being tried before a tribunal, which would lead to the final verdict—banishment.

But then again, maybe it wouldn't. Cassie's memory of what happened was already partially destroyed by Alister. Maybe, by the time his trial occurred, the memory wouldn't hold any evidence of Ronan's work. Maybe. But was he really willing to risk everything on that chance?

Islayne was his home, and lumination was his future. What could life possibly hold for him without those two things? He tried to think rationally. Though it wasn't required by law, his parents would move with him. He could apply to colleges, and his parents would get new teaching jobs. Eli, Cassie, and hopefully Adele would come visit him. They could call and text each other. It wouldn't be the same, but he wouldn't have to lose them completely.

But even as he tried to imagine a life outside of Islayne, his chest felt like it was caving in on itself. This island was in his blood. It was more than just the backdrop of his days; the woods and the sea and the massive sloping hills had woven themselves into the fabric of his being. People talked about putting down roots when they found a home, but to Ronan, it was the opposite. Islayne had rooted itself deeply into him, and it wasn't in his power to tear himself away.

And to be forced to watch his gifting die out? He would never find any other kind of work that would even come close to lumination. He would spend the rest of his life aimless and frustrated, never able to do the one thing that made him feel fulfilled. He wouldn't survive the loss of everything all at once—his home, his friends, his gifting. He would have nothing left. It couldn't happen. He couldn't let it happen.

"Ronan," Alister said softly, taking a small step closer to him. "I know how much this life means to you. Don't let it all slip away now. I promise no harm will come to you or the others. Let me take the memories of the past few weeks, and then everything can go back to normal. You can return to your apprenticeship. You can finally become a full-fledged luminator, and I will be able to enact all of the change that I know you want to see. You can stay here, on Islayne, for the rest of your life. Nothing will have to change. I can make everything right again. Just trust me."

Alister's words were weaving a sort of comfortable spell around Ronan. Would it be so bad, really, to have everything go back to the way it was a month ago? No one would know the difference. Ronan himself wouldn't know the difference. All of these recent discoveries would be part of a bad dream. And he could wake up to life the way it was supposed to be—learning how to be a luminator and living life on Islayne with his friends. Maybe Adele was right. Maybe, just this once, forgetting would be better.

But at that thought, something deep inside him broke through all of his fears and all of his justifications. He remembered why it would be so terrible to lose his gifting in the first place—because memories were sacred. He remembered the awe he felt when he brought Jillian's memory back from the point of extinction. He recalled the vibrancy of the colors and the brilliant mix of sounds and smells. He remembered what it felt like to breathe life back into something so close to dying. And then he remembered the agony of that piercing scream, and the painful ache in his heart as he watched Alister drain the scene of all life. He remembered the utter wrongness of it all. He could never be a part of that. He couldn't allow that to happen to his own memories, and he definitely couldn't allow that to happen to his friends.

"Go to hell," Ronan said.

But in his indecision, Ronan hadn't noticed Alister creeping slowly closer to him. As Ronan spoke, Alister knocked the gun out of his grasp and then threw him bodily to the floor. Ronan hit his head against a stone, and the room started tilting. He looked out at the cavern as Alister dragged him back and tossed him onto the metal table. Ronan tried to fight back, but he couldn't get his bearings, and the room refused to stop spinning. He felt Alister's meaty hands on his temples, luring him into the dream state. Ronan's last thought was that he must be hallucinating, because he could have sworn that Ben Roscoe was running toward him from the mouth of the cavern. Then the world faded to black.

24

Ronan woke up to the beeping of a machine and halfway hushed voices. His head was pounding, and his eyelids felt too heavy to open. Nothing seemed familiar to him, and his mind was in a fog. He forced his eyes open. The glare of the florescent bulbs was blinding. He caught sight of a speckled, tiled ceiling before he shut his eyes against the light. The unmistakable smell of sickness and antiseptic reached him, and he knew he was in a hospital. But why? He tried to recall the past few days, but nothing came to mind.

"Do you think he's milking this? Like, maybe he's secretly been awake for hours, but he just likes the excuse to lay around and not do anything?" Eli asked.

"Eli, shut up," Cassie said, her voice sounding much more strained than normal. "He hit his head really hard. The doctor said he could have brain damage."

At the sound of their voices, the scene from the cavern slowly came into focus in Ronan's mind. He felt panic rising in his chest. He sat up suddenly, trying to ignore how the movement shot a new throbbing pain into his skull.

"Did he do it?" he cried. "Did Alister destroy my memories?"

He looked back and forth between Eli, who looked like he was trying not to laugh, and Cassie, who looked sick with worry. They were sitting next to him. From the extra blankets draped across the arms of the chairs and their disheveled appearances, Ronan guessed that they'd been sleeping by his bed.

"I'm going to let you work through that one for yourself," Eli said.

"Stop teasing him, Eli, he's been through a lot," Cassie said. "No Ronan, we got to you in time."

Ronan suddenly felt foolish. Of course, if he remembered that Alister was going to murder his memories, then the man must not have succeeded.

"Oh, right," he said sheepishly. "But how did you guys get there so fast?"

"It was your crazy, reclusive boss, my very, *very*, distant cousin, who was our knight in shining armor," Eli told him. "He said you left your phone in his office. When you didn't come back, he got worried and read Cassie's text message to you. He drove over to her home and when no one answered the door, Ben decided to come in through a window and look around—something you must forget is not very socially acceptable when you spend the better part of fifteen years alone. Cassie heard someone come inside and started yelling for help. After he found us, it didn't take long to figure out where Alister was probably taking you. It was a close call though. By the time we reached the cavern, you were lying on a table and had blood gushing from your head. It looked like Alister was seconds away from starting a session. Luckily, Ben had brought his own gun, and once he told Alister that the Council enforcers were only a few minutes behind him, all of the fight went out of him."

Ronan saw Cassie flinch as Eli said her father's name. Ronan felt a pang of pity for her. He couldn't imagine what she must be feeling, knowing what her father had planned to do. But she looked exhausted and anxious, so he didn't think it was the right time to ask her how she was doing. Eli must have also noticed her stiffen beside him, because he moved on quickly.

"You were unconscious when we reached you, so we brought you back here and watched you take a nice long twenty-hour nap, and now you've finally decided to grace us with your presence again."

Ronan stomach tightened as he thought of how close he'd come to allowing Alister to erase his memories. Now sitting here, looking at Cassie and Eli, he realized how stupid and selfish he'd been to even consider it. But that didn't stop the dread from pooling in his stomach, weighing him down, as he realized what would happen now.

"Have you talked to the Council yet about submitting your memory for evidence?" Ronan asked.

The look that Cassie and Eli exchanged gave Ronan his answer.

"We've been taking shifts here," Cassie said. "When we first got back, Adele sat here with you, and Eli and I went to the Council. After what happened last time we waited, we didn't want to take any chances. Ronan, I'm so sorry. I didn't know they would have to launch a separate investigation into the illegal session you completed. Neither of us thought about it. We were so focused on making sure they found out the truth about my dad. It wasn't until we were in the middle of the official report with the Council secretary that we realized, and by then, it was too late..." She trailed off, looking completely miserable.

"We don't know anything for sure yet," Eli said gravely, all previous teasing forgotten. "They may not bring us up on the full charges, considering that we're helping to put Alister away. We won't know for a few weeks."

"I think we know, Eli," Ronan said softly, trying to keep edge out of his voice and almost succeeding. He had so many different emotions warring inside of him—remorse over what he'd almost done, sadness over Cassie's hurt, anger at what his life would be like now. But one thing was for sure, he wasn't in the mood for false comfort. The Council would charge him with illegal memory brightening, and just like in every other case on Islayne in the past fifty years, they would banish him from the island.

"Ronan, if I'd known that it would come to this," Cassie began.

"It's okay," he said, though nothing felt okay. But he had to say it because Cassie had enough to struggle with right now, and he wasn't going to make it even more difficult.

As if on some kind of cue, the pain in his head roared back to life. He lay back against the hospital bed, suddenly too exhausted to stay upright.

"I think I need more sleep—and more pain meds," he said. "Could you guys come back later?"

"Sure man, whatever you need," Eli said, standing up. Cassie leaned over and kissed him on the forehead. As they walked out the door, Ronan's head began to spin from everything that would change in the coming weeks. The nurse came in and gave him more painkillers. He closed his eyes, and mercifully, within a few minutes, he fell back to sleep.

25

Cassie deleted all of her social media accounts, and Adele's mum made sure the news was never on in the house. Cassie loved Gina for that. She didn't want to hear the outrage over her dad's actions repeated over and over again, and more than that, she didn't want to hear the latest vicious gossip about how she must have known and must have been protecting her father. She had enough to face without adding the judgment of people she'd never met.

Gina had come out to the island as soon as Adele told her what had happened. She made Cassie's home feel warmer and more inviting just by being there. Which was good, considering how Cassie wasn't leaving her house much these days. She could ignore the news and the internet, but that still didn't shield her from people coming up to her on the street or in the grocery store and accusing her of being complicit in her father's crimes. The first time it happened, she thought she would be furious, but instead it just made her feel exhausted and small. She didn't have the energy or the desire to correct anyone or to fight back. Instead, she began to only leave the house to visit Ronan in the hospital. Gina told her that it would blow over in time, and people wouldn't always be so angry. She said to be patient, but Cassie felt too tired for patience.

As she stepped out of the hospital doors after her latest visit to Ronan, she felt the increasingly familiar sense of guilt settle in her chest. It wasn't just over the illegal session that would most likely lead to Ronan's banishment. In fact, over the past two days of visiting, Ronan had told her multiple times that he wasn't upset with her, and she was beginning to believe him. But that was only the small, logical part of her guilt. More often, she felt blame for her DNA. She'd look at Ronan's nasty cut on the side of his head and feel a sinking sense of responsibility that the culprit's blood ran through her veins.

She knew intellectually that she wasn't accountable for her father's actions, but she wished her intellect had done more for her over the years. She should have realized what her father was capable of. She lived with the man day in and day out her whole life, and she'd never suspected anything. She'd been so blinded by hero worship and a longing for his approval, she'd never stopped to wonder whether he deserved it.

But deeper than any of these feelings—buried beneath the guilt and the frustration and the exhaustion—Cassie mourned the loss of her second parent, even as a part of her was angry at herself for feeling so bereft. Her father wasn't gone in the same way her mother was, but in her mind, it felt the same. She'd already decided not to visit him before the trial. It was too painful, and she didn't have anything to say to him. There was no chance he would escape banishment or imprisonment on the mainland. The trial would be over in a matter of weeks, and he would be gone.

"You know, if paramedics were trying to wheel in a dying man, where every second of delay brought him closer to the brink of his demise, you would feel really bad for standing in the middle of the doors and blocking their path."

Cassie smiled despite herself, glancing over to see Eli leaning against the wall of the hospital. Though his tone had been light, Cassie could see the concern in his eyes as he looked at her.

"They have a different entrance for emergencies," she retorted.

"Yes, but that would take longer to reach. Weren't you listening? My hypothetical patient is on the verge of death."

"I'm not sure causing the death of an innocent person could make me any less popular around here." Cassie had meant to say it flippantly, but she couldn't quite keep the bitter edge out of her voice.

Eli studied her for a moment. "Come on, let's take a drive," he said, inclining his head toward the car park. "I'll be your personal chauffeur and take you anywhere you feel like going. Sky's the limit."

"I hate that phrase. All those poor kids who want to be astronauts."

"Well in this case, it's perfectly accurate. We only have my car. No space travel."

"Then it's not actually accurate at all. More like, the ground's the limit."

"You're quickly losing your free ride," Eli said.

"Let's drive out to Tudic Lake."

As they made their way up the winding dirt roads, Cassie studied Eli from the passenger seat, trying to figure out what exactly was different about him. He seemed calmer and more sure of himself.

"Are you worried about the Council ruling?" Cassie asked.

Eli tilted his head to the side, weighing her question.

"For Ronan? Yes, very much. For me? No."

"Why?"

"Because I was doing some research on past Council cases, and the most that's ever happened to an apprentice who began an illegal session but didn't actually brighten anything was that they were stripped of their provisional license and banned from ever practicing lumination again."

She laughed incredulously. "And that's not enough to make you worried?"

He glanced over at her, as if deciding whether or not to tell her something.

"No, Cassie, it's not. It would be a relief to be done with the trade."

"What are you talking about? You've spent all this time working toward becoming a luminator."

"I didn't have a choice. It's kind of assumed, in my family, that if you have the gifting, that's what you do. You don't really have a lot of options."

"I never knew it wasn't what you wanted."

"I know," he said, sighing. "I've never told anyone, well except Ronan a few days ago. But that was an accident. I guess I thought...you would think less of me, if you knew. I never did anything about it because I didn't want to stand up to my parents and risk losing them. Now that this has come out, they aren't speaking to me yet, but they haven't completely disowned me either. I think they're going to come around, and I'll finally have the freedom to go do something that interests me."

"Like what?" she asked.

"I don't know, maybe a history professor, or something," he said lightly, as if it didn't matter. Cassie knew it did.

She nodded. "I could see that."

"Are you disappointed?" he asked. "You can be honest."

"Eli, come on, being honest with each other has never really been our issue. Of course I'm not disappointed. Why would I be? It's not like it was a prerequisite for our friendship."

"I could just always tell, even if you got annoyed when we talked about it too much, I could tell that you respected luminators. Especially your dad—" He stopped suddenly.

"It's okay," Cassie said. "I'm not going to fall apart if you mention him. But yeah, obviously being a luminator doesn't make you a good or bad person. You do whatever you want to do, Eli, it's not going to make me like you less. A lot of other things might, but not your career choice."

"Yeah? So you're saying that I could do anything as a career and it wouldn't change your opinion of me? Perfect, I think one of the leads of that kids' music group, the Wiggles, is retiring. Fame and fortune here I come."

"Don't push your luck."

They drove in comfortable silence for a few minutes, until Eli asked, "So, do you wanna talk about it?"

"About what?"

He gave her a knowing look.

"Oh, you mean about how my dad's a psychopath? Or wait, maybe about how I screwed up the life of one of my best friends? Or are you referring to how everyone on this island seems to hate me? There are so many potentially awesome conversation topics, it's hard to choose." Cassie leaned her head back against the seat and stared at the green blur of the forest rushing by the window.

"You know, I'm starting to wonder if it'd be better if I just...left," she said quietly.

Eli jerked back as if she'd hit him. "You're not seriously thinking that, are you?"

Cassie didn't look at him. "Gina is talking about trying to move here and work remotely. But maybe instead, I could go live with them on the mainland until I graduate. And then, maybe I could go to university in America. Somewhere far away from here, and far away from my dad."

"But Islayne is your home. How could you leave?"

"I don't want to spend the next several years around people who hate me because of my father. In some ways, I've lived in his shadow my whole life, Eli. I'm just wondering what it would be like to be free of that, to go somewhere new and start fresh. Where people would look at me and see me, instead of seeing him."

Eli was quiet for so long Cassie thought he wasn't going to respond at all. Then suddenly, he veered off onto a small side road, put the car in park, and turned to face her.

"I see you, Cassie," he said urgently. "I've seen you since the moment we met. I know that you are fearless and loyal and beautiful. I know that you wring more life out of a week than most people do in a year. And I know that this is the point where I'm supposed to tell you as your friend that I understand why you want to leave. I should say that I support you and that if you think leaving is best, then you should go.

"But I can't say that. And maybe it's selfish. Maybe it's because the thought of not getting to see you every week makes me feel like I'm drowning. Maybe it's because I can't imagine life on Islayne without you. But I think it's also because it's not in you to run away from hard things. I think if you leave now, you'll be miserable, knowing that you let other people rule your life like this.

"Don't go. Don't leave for me, but also, don't leave for you. I know this next year will be hard. But I'll be here, and Gina and Adele will be here. We'll be your family. Please don't leave."

Cassie closed her eyes and took a deep breath. She didn't know how to answer. The truth was, she wasn't sure she was as strong as Eli said. She wasn't sure she could handle this. She could still see the look of hatred on that woman's face who'd stopped her at the grocery store the other day.

When she thought of moving to the mainland, it felt like a weight was lifting off her chest. But maybe it wasn't the cure-all that she thought it would be. Even if she left, she would still have to deal with the truth about her father. She couldn't escape that, no matter where she went. And Eli was right, she hated the idea of letting other people's opinions control her actions. Could she really live with herself if she ran away? It was one thing to face the bad opinions of a crowd; it would be much harder, in the long run, to live with herself knowing she'd been a coward.

And if she left, she'd be leaving Eli behind. A fierce resistance rose up in her heart at the thought. No. She couldn't let that happen.

"Okay," she said finally, taking his hands. "I'll stay."

26

THE VERDICTS CAME SWIFTLY. AFTER TWO WEEKS OF COUNCIL investigations, Alister Murdoch was found guilty of gross misconduct, stripped of his license, banished from the island, and sentenced to fifteen years imprisonment on the mainland. One week later, Eli Brennington was found guilty of attempted illegal underage lumination and was stripped of his provisional license. Ronan Saunders was found guilty of actual illegal underage lumination and was sentenced to a lifetime of banishment from Islayne. Ben Roscoe stood in the small crowd in the upper level of the Council chambers when the third sentence was handed down to his apprentice. As soon as the judge spoke the words, Ben stood up and walked out of the building, not looking back to see Ronan's reaction to the news.

He held the manual firmly with one hand as he drove the old familiar road to his parents' estate, as if the book might disappear if he released it from his grasp. After all, these pages had eluded him for the past fifteen years. Fifteen years of searching the island, going to every yard and estate sale, paying off petty criminals to help him break into mansions and comb through every library. In his more dejected—or perhaps lucid—moments of searching, Ben wondered if his grandfather had been lying, if he was spending so much time and energy chasing a fantasy. But that thought could never seem to stay in his head. After a few days of swearing off the search,

Ben would close his eyes and see the blank look on his little brother's face, and so he never stopped the hunt for long. If only to keep his ghosts quiet.

Now after so many years, he finally held the book in his hands. He could feel the smooth worn pages and smell the leather cover. But it didn't matter. He slammed his other hand against the steering wheel in frustration.

Turn back! Turn back! A voice kept sounding in his head as the car made its way up the white stone driveway. Ben surveyed the immaculately manicured lawn and ornate fountains at the front of the mansion. A memory rose up unbidden in his mind. Five-year-old Jeremy raced in between the fountains as Ben chased him, laughing, pretending that his younger brother could outrun him. Then he crouched behind one of the bushes, and when Jeremy rounded the corner of the yard, Ben sprang out and surprised him. His little brother had been so startled that he crashed into one of the fountains, breaking his nose and getting blood all over the white marble. He remembered how his mother had fussed over Jeremy as she lectured Ben, but when she turned her back, they grinned at each other.

Ben shook his head as he parked the car, as if trying to dislodge the memory. That was the problem with coming back here. Everything held significance. He couldn't look at any piece of this mansion without a dozen painful recollections coming to mind, all leading back to Jeremy. He forced himself to focus on the task at hand, took a deep breath, and rang the doorbell.

The front door of his home had been stained a darker brown, and it threw him for a moment. Somehow, he thought nothing could change in this house once he left. There was part of him that had assumed that when he came here, everything would look the exact same as it had when he'd walked out fifteen years ago. Of course, that wasn't logical, but it still felt strange to see something in his old home.

The door swung open to reveal his father. The years had not been kind to him, and he looked even more weathered and hardened than he had on the day Ben told him that he blamed him for everything that had happened. On the day Ben walked away from this house and this life.

"I know why you're here." His father's tone was light and flippant, as if seeing his oldest son after so many years had no effect on him at all. Maybe it didn't. Ben had stopped trying to determine his father's feelings a long time ago.

"I doubt that," Ben responded.

"Come inside. I don't make a habit of having conversations in my doorway."

His father led him to the small study off the main foyer. The familiar smell of leather, cigars, and wood smoke filled Ben's senses. Growing up, he'd never been allowed in this room. It still felt off-limits to him, even though the fire was lit, and the scene looked inviting.

"You want to lecture me some more," his father said, coming around and sitting in one of the plush chairs by the fire. "You want to tell me how everything that has happened lately—with Murdoch and that upstart apprentice of yours—is also my fault."

"No, I'm here to tell you to fix it," Ben said, forcing himself to sit opposite his father.

"Oh, is that all? And how do you propose that I do that?"

"I want you to reverse the Council ruling, and allow Ronan Saunders to remain on the island and continue in his training."

His father made a derisive noise. "You've been away so long, you must have forgotten how these things work. I don't have that amount of influence, and the Council does not reverse its rulings. Ever. If you wanted to keep that little brat safe on the island, maybe you should have paid more attention to what he was doing in his free time."

"Don't lecture me on keeping people safe," Ben said.

"This is not about Jeremy."

"It's always about Jeremy," Ben said tiredly. "But I'm not here to discuss the past. I'm here to put it to bed." He held out the manual. It pained him to release his grip on the leather as his father took it from him. A part of him raged against what he was going to do. That book was meant to bring him justice. It wasn't a bargaining chip. But he had already decided; he wouldn't turn back now.

His father traced the front cover for a moment and then flipped through the pages. He finally looked back up at Ben.

"In the Council proceedings, they said the manual had never been recovered, that it disappeared after Alister was arrested."

"In a manner of speaking," Ben said. "Recognize the handwriting?"

"Of course I do."

"Good," Ben said with steel in his voice. He opened his mouth to say more, but the words refused to come. He was shaking with anger. Everything in him rebelled against this choice. There was still time. He could take this book to the Council. He could match the handwriting to letters from his grandfather. With that evidence, the Council would have cause to search Jeremy's mind, and then all secrets would be laid bare. This could still be the moment that Ben had dreamt of for so long. He could tell his father that he was finally revealing the sins of his family. He could repay his grandfather for all the lost moments with Jeremy, for the broken life the man had left in the wake of his ambition and his vicious curiosity. He could drag the Roscoe name through the mud, and then he would finally be able to sleep at night.

No. No. No. He had already decided. He would not let another person suffer on account of his family. He forced his mouth to form the words.

"If you do as I ask, then no one will ever know who authored this manual."

His father scowled at him. "You would dare blackmail me? Do you have no loyalty?"

Ben's eyes widened in disbelief. "Loyalty?! To this family? I have spent the last fifteen years looking for this book, hoping to expose all of you for what happened. Be thankful I have finally found a more worthy goal. Loyalty is only as good as its object. To say I have no loyalty to this family is to pay me a compliment."

"No one was as angry over what happened as I was, Benjamin. Do you know your mother still cries over it at night? But no good would have come from coming forward."

"You saw it happen! Your memory would have been enough evidence to convict him! He deserved to pay for his crimes. If only you'd cared more about your son than you did about your reputation."

"I will not sit here and be judged by you," his father said icily. He held up the manual. "Perhaps I'll just throw this in the fire and be done with it."

"You could, but I've spent the past several weeks staring at these pages. It would take a trained luminator a few hours, at most, to find a memory that showed the handwriting from this book clearly. That, combined with one of the many letters I still have from Grandfather would be more than enough to implicate him in the book's creation. To cement his guilt, I would hold Jeremy forth as evidence."

Now his father did look truly angry. "You wouldn't do it. It would kill your mother."

"I will do what is necessary. Don't force my hand."

"How do I know that you won't turn your memories of the book in after I speak to the Council?"

"Because that is the one way I am like you. I always keep my word."

His father was silent for a long time, staring into the fire. Finally, he turned back toward Ben. "I will do it."

Ben leaned over and took the book from his father's hands. He hesitated for the briefest of moments, and then before he could second-guess his decision again, he threw it into the fire. The flames licked at the pages eagerly, causing them to curl and blacken. Ben looked away and stood up to leave.

"Benjamin," his father said, rising also. "I know that you blame me. But you must know, I didn't mean for it to happen. I am sorry."

Ben studied his father's face for a moment. He thought he saw the slightest hint of true remorse in his rough features. "I believe you," he said as he walked toward the study doors. "But it's not enough."

As Ben walked toward his car, he stopped for a moment to look at the mansion one more time. A movement in the window of an upstairs bedroom caught his eye, and he saw a curtain pulled back. A young man stared down at him. Even at this distance, and even after so many years, he could easily recognize Jeremy's dark hair, round face, and slightly pointed ears. Ben took a step back toward the house—pulled instinctively toward his brother—but the look in Jeremy's eyes brought him up short. There was no hint of recognition there. Ben could have been anyone standing on the front lawn. The familiar weight of grief settled again on Ben's chest. He made sure not to look at the fountain as he drove away.

27

THREE DAYS LATER, RONAN WAS SAVORING THE SILENCE IN HIS HOME WITH both his parents out running errands. Ever since they'd come back from holiday right before the trial, Ronan felt like his life was rife with discussions about what had happened and what to do now and what housing was available and what new teaching jobs his parents could secure. Overall, they had been really supportive of him, and they were taking this unexpected turn in their lives much better than Ronan had expected. But he was still tired of the perpetual talking.

The sound of his doorbell broke into the quiet, and Ronan opened his front door to see Ben standing on his porch. He felt a stab of guilt that he hadn't ever stopped by to thank the man for saving him in the cavern. But seeing his trainer would only remind Ronan of the future that had slipped out of his grasp, and the guilt he felt was easier to bear than the pain of that reminder.

"You seem recovered enough," Ben said, walking into Ronan's house without waiting for an invitation.

"Ben, listen, I've been meaning to thank you for saving me—"

Ben held up his hand to stop Ronan. "I'd like to know what could possibly be the reason that you've been shirking your apprenticeship. Like the taste of time off too much? Decided on a different trade? Couldn't take the pressure of comparing your work with mine?"

"My apprenticeship? But I just assumed..."

"That what? A little time in the hospital was excuse enough for almost a month of holiday?"

"No," Ronan said, overcoming his surprise and getting frustrated now. Why was Ben making him rehash all of this? When his parents weren't making him talk about it, Ronan tried to avoid thinking about it as much as possible because the only other course of action was to let the Council verdict rule his mind every moment of every day, sinking him into depression and making him miss out on the few precious days he had left on Islayne.

"I can't practice any longer. Are you living under a rock? Didn't you hear about the Council ruling? They stripped me of my provisional license, and I only have another three weeks on the island before I have to leave."

Ben exhaled impatiently. "That's what this is all about? I've been having to do my own cleaning over that? Did I forget to give this to you? Wait a second, where is that note?"

After digging around in his pocket for a moment, Ben finally pulled out a wrinkled letter and handed it to Ronan. It bore the Council's official seal.

"They asked me to deliver it to you myself. Like I'm your messenger boy, or something," Ben said. Ronan could tell that he was faking his annoyance.

The Council's recent ruling has been overturned...

The evidence has been found inadmissible according to regulation 45-b...

Your provisional license has been reinstated...

The words swam on the page. His mind was having trouble comprehending the reality

of what he was reading. Ronan looked up at Ben.

"I...I don't have to leave? I can still practice?" he asked.

"There's that conventional intelligence at work," Ben said.

There was a part of Ronan that refused to be taken in by Ben's words. Even as a spark of hope lit in his chest, that other part of him wanted to crush it. Because if he began to believe he didn't have to leave—if he thought it was possible to wake up a month from now in his own home, with Cassie, Eli, and Adele only a few miles away, with a future of lumination still within reach—and it turned out to be a lie, he didn't think he would ever recover.

"It doesn't make any sense. The Council never overturns their rulings. Why would they do it for me?"

"Why does it matter? I thought you'd be happy about it," Ben said.

"I am, but...I don't think I'll be able to believe it until I know why."

Ben sighed dramatically and then sat down on one of the stools at the island counter.

"I used Alister's manual to blackmail my father into using his influence with the Council to overturn your sentence."

Ronan stared at him, at a total loss for words.

"You might want to sit down," Ben said. "You once asked me about my family. You mentioned my grandfather, Adrian, on the first day of your apprenticeship. He was a brilliant luminator in his day. But by the time I was old enough to know him, he had already lost much of his memory and personality to dementia. An ironic end, I always thought, considering luminators, for all our gifting, have no power over that disease. He still had moments of being completely lucid, but most of the time, he would just ramble on about people and things unintelligibly. Though I have to say that I almost preferred the times when he wasn't coherent. He might have been good at his work, but he was a stodgy, arrogant, hard old man.

One day, I was eating lunch with him—something my father forced me to do at least once a week, perhaps to assuage his own guilt over barely spending time with the man. My grandfather began to tell me that after a while, he tired of simply being the best luminator on Islayne. He said that he needed a new way to challenge himself, so he began to toy with different techniques.

Instead of healing memories, he tried to find ways to manipulate them. He began to find people to experiment on, testing out the different powers of his mind. How he got away with this for so long, I can't be sure, but I can only assume that family prestige and wealth shielded him from the eyes of others. And, of course, the Council wasn't as watchful in those days as it is now.

"I'll never forget the way his face looked when he told me that eventually, he'd discovered a way to destroy memories altogether. He seemed so proud of what he had accomplished. And he told me that some days, all he could think about was getting the chance to use his new ability at least once more before he died.

"He said that while he wanted his legacy to live on after him, he was not foolish enough to broadcast what he had found. So, he decided to create a manual that contained the knowledge he'd discovered, but he wrote it in Classical Gaelic—something my family has been taught for generations. Don't ask me why. It always seemed like a pointless waste of time to me.

"After that disturbing conversation, I related everything I'd learned to my father. But he dismissed it out of hand as the crazy ramblings of an old man. I tried to convince him that my grandfather had been coherent during the conversation, but it was no use. As time went on, I began to convince myself that my father was right, and that my grandfather had either been out of his mind or outright lying to me.

"Then, one day, a few months later, when I'd been sent again to eat lunch with my grandfather, I couldn't find him anywhere in our home. As I looked in every room, it became clear that my youngest brother, Jeremy, who was only eight years old at the time, was also missing. Eventually, my whole family joined in the search for him, and my father was the one who finally found him. I heard his cries emanating from the empty back wing of our mansion. A few moments later, I rushed into the room to see Jeremy lying prone on the dusty floor of the deserted ballroom, and my grandfather was wandering around the room aimlessly.

"Jeremy didn't wake up for two days, and when he did, he had no memory of me, my parents, or his life on Islayne. But not only was his past lost to him, he also had trouble forming any new memories. I would tell him who I was, and then an hour later, he had forgotten again. After weeks of this, with nothing changing, I begged my parents to take him to a luminator to see if anything could be done, but they refused. They were too worried about rumors spreading.

"So finally, I decided to do an illegal session on him, just to see if I could help. I'd only been apprenticed for a few months, and I knew it was a foolish thing to do, but I felt as though I had no other choice. Much like you may have felt, perhaps. When I pulled the mindscape out of his head, what I saw was...sickening. It was as if all of his memories were diseased. I could only conclude that whatever my grandfather had done in destroying a few memories had spread like some kind of contagion to the rest of them. Nothing in my brother's condition has changed in the years since."

"What?!" Ronan interrupted, too startled to care about being rude. "You're saying that every time your grandfather, or Alister, destroyed a scene in someone's mind, that it didn't stop there? That it wrecked the victim's entire memory?"

"Yes, that's what I believe. It was true of my brother, at any rate."

Ronan felt like he couldn't breathe. If Ben hadn't rescued him, he wouldn't just have lost selective scenes from this summer, he would have lost...everything. And not just him, but Cassie, Eli, and Adele, too. He shuddered. Had Alister known? No. Ronan couldn't believe he did. But still, to know how close they'd come to that fate. He shut his eyes for a moment and placed his hands flat on the island counter, trying to steady himself.

"I didn't think about that being news to you, but of course it would be," Ben said gently. Ronan wasn't used to his trainer speaking to him in that tone.

"It's okay...I'm just trying to come to terms with it. But then, why would Cassie still have a functioning memory?"

Ben nodded. "I'd wondered that myself. I think it must be because Alister didn't go through with it. Since he stopped before that one scene was fully erased, it must have kept the rest of her memory intact."

Ronan considered Ben's words for a moment. It made a kind of sense. He thought of how Alister would feel knowing how close he'd come to wrecking his own daughter's memories not once, but twice. Ronan wondered if he would even care.

"I'm sorry I interrupted. You can keep going."

Ben nodded.

"I told my father that Adrian had done this, and I was furious with him for dismissing my earlier concerns. I told him that I wanted Adrian brought up on charges with the Council. My father wouldn't hear of it. I spent the next week combing through our family library, but the manual he'd written was nowhere to be found. My father and I had another massive quarrel over bringing Adrian before the Council, and then afterwards, I left. I've spent the intervening years fruitlessly searching for that book, hoping to find it and use it to expose my grandfather's actions. Then you mentioned writing in Classical Gaelic and promptly disappeared. I was worried about you, but I also thought that just maybe, you had somehow stumbled upon the book. And it turns out I was right."

"When I found your friends, Eli told me about the manual you all had discovered and about Cassie's memory. I recalled that, years before he had made any headway as a luminator, Alister used to clean my parents' home on the side for extra income. I can only assume that he found the book in our library and took it."

"And you were the one to take it from the cavern?" Ronan asked.

Ben nodded.

"Where is it now?"

"When my father promised to use his influence with the Council to secure your future, I burned the manual, as we agreed. A fair trade."

Ronan was stunned. He stared at Ben. "After so many years of searching, you gave that up for me?"

"It was time that no one else suffered for the sins of my family."

"I...I can't believe you would do that."

"Please don't start crying."

"I don't know what to say. Thank you."

"Yes, well, you can repay me by starting to pay better attention and not making any more stupid mistakes. And no more illegal memory sessions."

"It's a deal," Ronan said, and he realized he was grinning for the first time in weeks. Ronan decided to push his luck with Ben in such a sharing mood. "Can I ask you something? Why did you decide to train me?"

Ben considered his question for a moment. "This trade was essentially handed to me on a silver platter. I didn't truly know what it was like to fight to make a living in this work until I cut ties with my family and the privilege that came with the Roscoe name. And even since that time, I know it's still easier for me to get clients than for the rest of the new luminators. I'm guessing that my father may have had a hand in that. I justified my privilege to myself by using the extra time and money to look for my grandfather's book. But still, I saw how high the deck was stacked against new luminators, and after so many years, I guess I was tired of doing nothing about it. So I decided to train you. It was a small thing, but at least it was something."

"With everything that's happened, do you think that any other new luminator will be able to win a Council seat this year?"

Ben sighed. "No. With Alister's recent disgrace, my relatives are going to do everything in their power to monopolize their grip on the trade. It will continue to be hard for new luminators to make a living. But many have been able to do it for years. Good things are often the most difficult to attain.

"Those who truly want to practice the trade will find a way to do it, no matter the obstacles in their way. And eventually, the old families won't have such a stranglehold on the Council. It's only a matter of time before a new luminator rises to the prestige of Alister Murdoch, and rises fairly. Who knows, it could be you."

Ronan thought back to what Alister had told him in the cavern about the corruption of the old families. He remembered the Academy students completely disregarding Alister, while the teachers looked on and did nothing. He recalled the frustration he felt in applying to every luminator on the island, only to be rejected time and again. Kendrick's face rose up in Ronan's mind, smug and delighted, as he gave Ronan the Council letter invalidating his apprenticeship. *One day,* Ronan thought. *I will make this trade better.*

"Now," Ben said, rising from the stool and starting for the door. "You have no more excuses for missing any more days of your apprenticeship. So you better be at the office first thing tomorrow morning. We have a new client. It should be interesting. And I lied about doing my own cleaning. You should probably get there a few hours early to make sure you have enough time to get things in order before we open."

28

THE NEXT EVENING, AFTER A WHOLLY EXHAUSTING DAY AT HIS apprenticeship, Ronan opened his postbox to see another scrawled note. This handwriting he'd know anywhere.

Meet us at 9 p.m. The beach closest to your house. Wear a swimsuit.

Cassie had planned their next summer excursion. Since her senior year would be starting in just a few weeks, Ronan had a hunch she would be cramming as much into these last few days as possible. He wasn't sure if he should take this as a good sign that she was coping well or a bad sign that she was using these as a distraction and not working through things at all. He hoped it was the former. In the days after he was released from the hospital, Cassie had tiptoed around him, doing anything he asked and apologizing over everything. It was exhausting and annoying. Ronan finally decided that enough was enough, so the next time he saw her, Ronan made sure to use every opportunity to make fun of her. After about half an hour of that, Cassie finally exploded in her normal spit-fire way. And since then, things had gone back to normal.

Ronan got to the beachfront exactly at 9 p.m., and once again, Cassie was nowhere in sight. *One day,* he said to himself, *I will remember to come thirty minutes later than she says.*

But someone else was there on time as well. Adele sat in the sand a few hundred feet from Ronan. Since visiting him in the hospital, Ronan had barely seen Adele. She'd seemed to go back to her old pattern of avoiding or ignoring him.

"So we were the suckers who got here right at nine," Ronan said, trying to sound casual, as he walked over to her.

She looked up and then away, as if she was disappointed. "I've been here for twenty minutes. You're slacking," she said.

"You're new to the group. The excitement will fade," he said, sitting down next to her. "How did you get here without Cassie?"

She shrugged. "I walked."

"It's over three miles!"

"It's fresh air. It's good for you."

"If you say so," Ronan said, tracing the sand absently. "So how's it going, with your mum here and everything?"

Adele looked out over the water for a moment. Ronan noticed how the moon shone off her dark brown curls. "I think you were right, about why I was angry," she said. "My mum and I talked about it. I do think my parents are going to get divorced, and it's still a lot to process, but I think at least my mum and I are okay now. It helps."

He nodded. "I am often right," he said. "It's good to know someone is finally noticing."

She laughed and shoved him lightly, but then Ronan noticed her inch just slightly away from him. Maybe it was that he'd gotten his life back in the past twenty-four hours, or that Ben had legitimately complimented his abilities that afternoon, or that he was just tired of wondering what she felt for him, but whatever the reason, he decided it was time to find out what was going on.

"Okay, I just have to ask you something. Why does your opinion of me seem to change from day to day?"

"What do you mean?"

"When we went kayaking, you seemed to warm up to me, but then the next time I saw you, you ignored me. The same thing happened the first time we explored the cavern. We had a great conversation, but then you went all cold again. When we were at the Roscoes' mansion, I thought we had a moment there, before we were interrupted. And you came to visit me in the hospital, but since then you've been avoiding me again. It's been bugging me ever since you got here, and I'm tired of it. What is going on?"

"I'm not...it's not...it's just complicated," she said, blowing out her breath in frustration. "Why do you care anyways?"

"Why do I care?" Ronan asked incredulously. "Because I *like* you, Adele. And it seems like half the time, you return the feeling, and half the time, you wished I didn't exist."

"I don't wish that," she said softly.

"Then what's the problem?" he asked.

"Were you listening to me at all the night of the party? My parents are going through a divorce, Ronan. And part of that is because my dad is gone all of the time. He barely ever sees my mom. I have witnessed the effects of two people who don't live most of their lives in the same place. I have the proof of what distance does to relationships. It kills them. You live here, and I live a three-hour ferry ride away from here, so how would that work exactly? It wouldn't, trust me. So yes, maybe I was trying to avoid you, to avoid something worse happening later."

"But you don't know that," Ronan said. "We aren't your parents. You said they had a lot of other problems. And besides, you are going to be here for a while."

"But probably not forever. I don't know if my mum can work from here yet, and she still doesn't know if I can get enrolled in school."

"So since we don't have a fool-proof guarantee of things working out, we aren't even going to give this a try?"

"It's not...I just don't think it will work..." She looked down at the sand.

"Do you want this to work?" Ronan asked, putting his hand on hers.

She froze, and for a moment, Ronan thought she was going to pull away, but then she nodded. "Yeah, I do, I want it to work."

"Okay then, let's give it a shot."

She held his gaze for another moment, looking torn by indecision. Then, she slowly leaned over and kissed him. Her lips were soft and full, and he felt like he could easily spend the next several hours doing exactly this.

"We can't leave you two alone for five minutes, can we?" Eli asked. Ronan broke away from Adele to see Eli and Cassie looking down at them. Adele ducked her head and blushed.

"Oh, wait, what's that excuse you used before, at the party, that no one really bought?" Ronan asked. "At least I own what I do."

"Ha, ha, very funny," Cassie said. "But you guys can kiss later. I have something awesome planned for tonight."

They got up and started to follow Cassie and Eli down the beach, Ronan keeping hold of Adele's hand. He looked out to see the moon's rippling reflection on the ocean waves. It was turning out to be a decent summer, after all.

THE END

ACKNOWLEDGMENTS

Book-writing is a crazy, fun, and often arduous adventure. I'm so grateful for the many people who came along for part or all of the journey.

Thank you to everyone who gave me feedback on painfully early drafts of this novel: David Bussell, Kristi Bussell, Samantha Bussell, Steve Bussell, Kelsey Gray, Alona Kosenko, Michelle Lloyd, Emily McGuire, Caitlin Rantala, Sarah Tiren, Diane Tyndall, and Kurt West.

A big thank you to my mom, Anne Bussell, for reading several iterations of this story and lending her finely tuned editing skills to whip the writing into shape.

To my daughters, Eliana and Riley, for teaching me much—sometimes more than I wanted—about balance, joy, and the importance of doing hard and beautiful things.

And most importantly, to my husband, Jason. Without you, this story would still be a blinking cursor on a blank screen.

Made in the USA
Middletown, DE
04 October 2017